# Heroin

## *Heartbreak*

♥♥♥♥

Vanessa M. Kirby

# ✿Acknowledgements✿

As always, I must first thank God once again for never failing me. Every day he makes his presence in my life known and for that I am thankful.

I'd like to thank the Clarke Family, especially Annemarie Clarke for having the courage to allow others to be a part of something so personal all in the name of saving one family from the heartache they have suffered through this past year. I know your suffering and pain will never end, but I pray that through this fictional tale you will be able to get your message out to others and with that find peace. Amber will now live in the hearts and minds of every person that opens this book.

Nicole Clarke, I just want to thank you for

having the courage to read these pages over and over again as we tried to make this story the best it could be. I know this wasn't easy and it will always be appreciated.

I'd like to say thank you to my husband who has been my biggest supporter through each of my projects. For always allowing me time and space even when it meant sacrificing our time together. I love you.

To my son, Jamal and my granddaughters, Zyanai and Zylah, I hope this project will be something that you can be proud of for years to come. I love you all very much.

To my mom, Annie, my sister, Danielle and my nephews, Antwyne and Alphonso thanks for your support. Alphonso, thanks for allowing me to include one of your many great poems in this story. I love you, Eboney and Zyaire. Thanks for serving your country in the United States Marine Corp.

To mom #2, Carrie, thank you for always supporting me. This year we suffered a terrible loss when my "Popi" left us to be with the Lord but the blessing he sent back will carry us through. Stacey, thank you for always having my back and giving words of encouragement. Your blessing will be arriving soon and I can't wait to be a part of your miracle.

To William (Big Will) Durant, you are the best test reader a girl can ask for. Your input and words of encouragement have always been a blessing since my very first project. Thanks for spreading the word, buddy.

To the rest of my family and friends, thank you all for the support you have shown throughout my writing career. I am stepping out on faith once again with something a little different than the norm, and I pray that you will embrace it as you have done all my other projects.

And last, but definitely not least, I want to thank Author Tammy Capri and the Nu Class Publications family for welcoming me into their circle and having faith in me and this project. I look forward to adding to the great empire you are building. Together we will achieve great things.

VANESSA M. KIRBY

# ❧Introduction❧

Today makes forty-seven days that I've been clean and sober. I really hope I can make it. I'm so lost and confused, but I don't understand why. I just want to be able to fucking love myself, and I feel like that day will never come. I really need help; I'm so sick. I guess that's all we addicts really are: sick people. I mean, who would find enjoyment out of sticking a needle in their arm and bobbing their head for a few hours while losing everything and everyone around them. People don't know what sick is, but I do. I got so much enjoyment out of those things; it was my life. I didn't need feelings, family, friends, or support. I just needed that little bag of powder. It's unbelievable how such a small thing can take over your life so quickly and how willing you become in letting it do so. Sick. Sick. Sick.

It's even sicker to think that even though I know nothing positive can come out of picking this shit up, I still want it more than anything. I have the disease of addiction, and it's rattling inside of my brain waiting to be let out of its cage. It will always be a constant battle, but I will never give up; I can't give up. The day I can give up the fight is the day I'm cured, and that may very well be the day I'm in the ground...

-Ashley

# ❧Chapter One☙

"Ashley, I need to know what's bothering you so I can help you," Dr. Schultz repeated when I didn't respond the first time.

"You asked me to get you some help, Ashley, and I did. But, it's pointless if you don't open up and tell Dr. Schultz what you told me," Aunt Chris pleaded with me.

I continued to stare from one to the other, while contemplating if this was the right decision after all. The other night when Aunt Chris figured out what had been eating at me all these years, it was a relief to finally be able to tell someone. I had spent many nights running from the monster in the closet, and I was tired of running. When she asked if I wanted to talk to someone about it, I said yes at the time. Now that we were sitting in the doctor's office, I just couldn't seem to make the words leave my mouth. They continued staring at me, waiting for me to say something. I had kept it bottled up for so long that I didn't know where to begin.

"Dr. Schultz, can I have a moment alone with Ashley?"

"Okay, but we only have another twenty minutes before the session will be over," she reminded Aunt Chris as she rose from her black swivel chair and headed for the door.

Once the door closed, Aunt Chris scooted closer to me, moved my long brunette hair out the way, took my hands in hers, and looked me dead in my big brown eyes. She always did this when we had our heart-to-heart talks. If I looked away, she knew I was not being truthful with her.

"Ash, do you want him to pay for what he did to you?"

"Yes," I responded with no hesitation.

My vision became blurred by the tears that immediately sprung forth, but I didn't look away. There was nothing I wanted more than to make him pay for the pain he had inflicted on me. I wanted to tell Dr. Schultz, but I was afraid she would judge me. I knew she would wonder why I waited almost twelve years to reveal this horrible truth. Honestly, I would've taken it to my grave if I could have, but I guess God felt I had suffered enough.

"Today is the day, Ash. Get it off your chest. Place the blame exactly where it lies...on him. Okay?"

Instead of answering verbally, I just nodded my head in agreement while using the balled up tissue I pulled from my blue hoodie to wipe my eyes. It's not like I hadn't relived this nightmare over and over again since it began when I was just five years old. I just didn't know how to tell someone else about it. The only reason I told Aunt Chris was because I actually came face to face with him that day. Seeing him made me feel like I was right back in that room fighting for my life. I prayed someone would come help me, but they never did.

*Is telling someone really going to help me now?*

Aunt Chris returned from summoning Dr. Schultz back into the room. I was so lost in my own thoughts I didn't even notice she had left. Dr. Schultz didn't return to her seat behind her massive oak desk filled with smiling family photos on one side and manila folders containing information of fucked-up people like me on the other. Instead, she took a seat on the couch on the opposite side of me. Now, I was sandwiched between her and Aunt Chris.

"Are you ready, Ashley?" she asked, using Aunt Chris' tactic of eye contact.

I nodded my head yes and pulled the hood of my jacket over my head, something I always do when I don't want people to see me. It makes me feel protected.

I took a few deep breaths to calm the butterflies in my stomach, cleared my throat, and then released the demon that had been controlling my life for years. It had turned me into something I never thought I'd be, something my family had no idea about...a heroin addict. I didn't reveal that, though. I just told them about *him*.

"My father molested me," I whispered and the tears immediately fell in quick succession.

The intercom on Dr. Schultz's desk buzzed at that moment.

"Dr. Schultz, your next patient has arrived."

I jumped up from the sofa and headed for the door. *I'm not so sure this was a good idea. I mean, what could she really do that getting high doesn't already do for me? Any fix is only temporary, so why not let it be one that at least makes me feel good for a while?*

"Will I see you next week, Ashley?" she called after me.

"I guess so," I mumbled, while thinking, *Don't hold your breath*, and kept walking.

# ❧Chapter Two❧

"So, Ash, are you going to ask your grandmom or what?" my girl Stacey asked for what seemed like the fiftieth time in the ten minutes we had been on the phone.

"I'm thinking about what to say," I replied, while pulling up my grey Victoria Secret sweatpants with the word LOVE written across the butt in pink letters. "You know she was pissed with me the last time I borrowed her car and didn't bring it back on time."

"I *really* need to get to Jake's," Stacey moaned, her high-pitched voice sounding like she was on the verge of crying.

"I know. Me, too. I'm all out, and after what I went through yesterday, I need more...desperately. Let me try something. If I don't call back in five minutes, then you know I'm on my way," I assured her, as I put on the matching top to my sweatpants while using my shoulder to hold my cell phone to my ear.

"Alright. Give one of your Emmy Award-winning performances," she encouraged. "You can do it. I have faith in you."

"Bye." I laughed as I hit the end button on my cell and stuffed it into my pocket.

Stacey had no idea just how good of a performer I could be. No one in my family knew about my favorite pastime, which was getting high. They also had no idea of my daily struggles because I hid it well. Daddy's betrayal had only been the beginning of my troubles. Every guy I'd been with had only escalated the self-hatred I felt. There was only one man in my life that gave me the love and security I needed, and that man was my Pop-Pop. No matter what my birth certificate said, he was the dad in my life.

"It's show time," I said.

I put on my grey Nikes with the pink soles, then grabbed my silver wallet and keys before heading downstairs. I walked in the kitchen and found Mom-Mom Nicolette standing at the stove preparing dinner. She's beautiful and quite feisty for her sixty-nine years. My friends never believed how old she was with her barely five-foot frame that weighed no more than a hundred and twenty-five pounds. Her gray hair styled in a bob with wispy bangs touching the tops of her eyelids was the only true hint that she's getting up in age.

Her hand swiped at the hair that was in need of a trim as she bustled about making her famous homemade sauce. No jars of Ragu for her; she made her sauce the old-fashioned way, along with jumbo-sized handmade meatballs and freshly made penne pasta that she purchased from a local neighborhood store.

Dinnertime was family time at Mom-Mom's. She was adamant about everyone eating together at the table for quality family time. It didn't matter to her that everyone had their own house. To her, this was home for all of us. My mom, Marie, would come by after work, and my stepdad, Jimmy, met her at Mom-Mom's with my little brother, Timmy. Aunt Christine and her new husband, Scott, were always there, and of course, Pop-Pop Howard. Yeah, we're one big happy family. Dinner was always at six o'clock sharp and usually lasted at least an hour or two, with the sharing of storytelling before everyone headed home.

With dinnertime a few hours away, Stacey and I desperately needed to see Jake. So, after pacing around the kitchen, opening and closing the refrigerator and cabinets like I was looking for something, I gathered the courage to ask Mom-Mom for her car. I walked up behind her and placed my hands around her waist, giving her a little squeeze.

"You must want something," she said with a chuckle.

"Mom-Mom, can I borrow your car to take Stacey to her doctor's appointment?"

She abruptly stopped stirring her sauce and turned to look at me. After what seemed like forever, she fixed her lips to speak.

"Before you say no," I quickly jumped in, "I know last time I was late, but I promise—"

"I don't know, Ashley," Mom-Mom said, cutting me off. "You don't know how to tell time," she added, then turned back to stir the food brewing on the stove.

"Please, Mom-Mom. I promise I'll take her and come right back," I assured her, while leaning on the counter next to the stove. "That night, I lost track of time celebrating with my friends. I was just so excited to have gotten my license."

I tilted my head to the side and gave her my best sweet-little-girl face that used to work so well. Now, it didn't seem to work like it did when I *was* that sweet little girl.

She covered the pot and turned to me. "Ashley, I have to pick your brother up from daycare at four o'clock."

"That's perfect. Stacey's appointment is at two-fifteen. It's an emergency appointment at Delaware County Memorial Hospital, which you know is a hop, skip, and jump from here," I joked.

She rolled her eyes up to the clock hanging on the wall. "It's quarter to two now," she said as she reached across the kitchen table for her pocketbook. "Please be back no later than three-thirty so I don't have to rush to get Timmy."

I held in my excitement as she handed me the car keys.

"Mom-Mom, I will." I gave her a quick peck on the cheek in appreciation.

"If you let me down, Ashley, this will be the last time—"

I didn't give her a chance to finish the statement. "I won't," I yelled back as I ran out the door.

I jumped into her green Kia Optima, jammed the key in the ignition, and pulled away before she could make it to the door to say anything else.

I drove the five blocks to Stacey's house in Drexel Hill, and just as I expected, she was waiting on her front porch. I tooted the horn, and like a kid in a candy store, she bolted down the steps.

"I can't believe you got the car! I guess you gave one hell of a performance," Stacey excitingly said as she slid her thin, five-foot-nine frame into the passenger seat.

She pulled up on the lever under the seat, pushing it back to make room for her long legs. Her long, wavy, jet-black hair was the only thing neat on her. The wrinkled blue t-shirt and jeans that had just as many stains as wrinkles told me that she was in one of her *"I don't give a shit"* moods. The toes that were in desperate need of a pedicure and peeking out the top of her slides confirmed my thoughts. Stacey may have liked to get high, but she usually prided herself on her appearance. The look she sported told me that she needed her fix bad.

As we pulled away from her house, she lit up a cigarette with shaky hands.

"I told her that I was taking you to your doctor's appointment," I said, hitting the button to roll down the window.

Mom-Mom would flip if her car smelled like cigarettes when I took it back. It would give her one more reason to hesitate the next time I asked to use the car.

"Ooh, you little liar." Stacey laughed as she took a deep drag on her Marlboro.

Her burnt fingertips caught my eye. She must've been smoking weed, something she always had on hand.

"Well, he does make us feel better, so it's not exactly a lie," I reasoned, laughing at my own joke as we arrived and parked around the corner from Jake's house.

He lived across the street from the hospital, so I did go where I said I was going...kind of.

Jake's house was a beautiful single home with a well-manicured lawn, winding driveway, and two-car garage in the rear; not exactly what you think of when you say the words "drug house". I guess that's because it was his parents' house, and they had no idea their soon-to-be college graduate was the biggest drug dealer on the campus of Delaware County Community College.

We rang the bell on the side of the house that granted entry to the basement where he stayed. It was like Fort Knox, with a security screen and a steel door. Also, there was one window at ground level, but it had that type of cinder block glass where you couldn't see inside. With all the money he was surely pulling in, I couldn't understand why he lived in his parents' basement, but to each his own.

Jake opened the inside door and then the security door, which required a key. After letting us in and locking it again, he went back to packing up our little goodie bag.

"What's up?" he asked as he continued counting the pills I assumed were for Stacey.

"Nothing," we replied in unison, while grabbing a seat at the opposite end of the bar from where he stood.

The first time I saw Jake, my mouth fell open; he was hot. I don't know what I expected a drug dealer to look like, but it wasn't that. I called him my *Almond Joy*. His skin tone was a sexy caramel as if he spent many hours in the tanning salon. His height was average, but the muscles seemed to pop from everywhere. I could tell his body was a temple, which made what he was doing seem so odd. His dark hair, which he kept cut close, made the color of his eyes appear even darker. As sexy as he was, he had a sinister look about him. You'd definitely think twice about crossing him.

I looked around, and just like the first time we came, I found myself amazed at how he had the basement hooked up. It looked like a studio apartment. There was a black leather sofa and love seat on one side of the massive space, a black and gold glass coffee table strategically placed in between the two, a full-size bar with a granite countertop, and four silver high-back stools with black leather seats. There was also an apartment-sized refrigerator and what looked to be a 65-inch TV with a surround sound system. The bedroom area was blocked off from view, and the small bathroom included a shower stall. The only thing he needed to go upstairs for was to cook, if he did, and use the laundry facilities that he mentioned were in a separate room upstairs. Plush carpet covered the floor and art hung on the walls. From the looks of the place, it didn't seem he would be moving out any time soon.

"What's up over at Upper Darby High?" he asked, making small conversation while finishing up our order.

"Nothing much. Same ole' shit," Stacey answered. "Nothing has really changed since you left."

"I just can't wait for graduation. You know I finished up my classes in January," I bragged, thinking it would impress him.

"Oh, you one of the smart ones, huh?" he said without taking his eyes off the pills.

"Yeah, I guess I am," I responded, thinking I scored some points.

"Can't be that smart if you're fucking with shit," he commented as he slid my bag down the bar to me.

Without bothering to respond, I slid the crumpled money I had been holding in my palm over to him and then gave him the middle finger.

"Keeps me in business, so I don't give a fuck what you do. As long as you have my money, you can get all the shit you want." He shrugged.

Yeah, he was fine as hell, but his attitude sucked!

"Well, as long as—"

The banging on the door interrupted Stacey, scaring the shit out of us. I guess our time was up, because Jake never let his customers inside his place at the same time. I guess it was for safety reason or maybe he didn't want anyone deciding to get together and rat him out if things went bad. I'm sure his parents wouldn't take kindly to having their home raided by the police and featured on the evening edition of the news.

He tried to finish packing Stacey's bag, but dropped the baggie before he was able to seal it. Pills scattered all over the floor. As the knock became more persistent, Jake went over and peeked through the hole in the door.

"Shit!" he spat. "What the fuck are they doing here?"

Jake looked back and forth from the door to the pills on the floor in agitation.

"Can you come back later?" he asked Stacey.

"Hell no! I need this shit now. Besides, I won't have a ride later."

Having no choice as the knocking got louder, Jake grabbed his keys and unlocked the door, but not before I noticed him pick up a gun from under the bar and stuff it in the back of his waistband.

Standing there were two gentlemen who looked like something out of a mob movie. Standing in commanding postures, both men were wearing dress pants and buttoned-down shirts with the collar open, allowing their gold chains and chest hair to be visible. Italian loafers and leather jackets completed their ensembles, even though the late-April temperature was a little too mild for leather.

"Max. Wayne," Jake said, acknowledging the gentlemen.

As soon as they entered, I noticed Jake's whole demeanor changed. He looked over at us and back at his pop-up guest; there would be no introductions. They remained in the doorway, not allowing Jake to lock the door.

"Let me clean this up and get them out of here," he told them, motioning to the spilled pills on the floor.

They didn't seem to be phased by the scattered drugs, but Jake's demeanor changed immediately. He looked as if he was beginning to suffocate, which was unusual since the temperature in the room was damn near freezing. His face turned a flushed red tint, and he suddenly started sweating profusely. That along with the fact that I knew he had a gun on him was my cue to get the hell out of there. Their mere presence put me in panic mode.

I nudged Stacey with my elbow and grabbed my stuff with the other hand. As soon as Jake refilled a new bag of Percocet for Stacey, we quickly headed for the door, which the two men continued to block with their enormous size. They reminded me of Big Pussy on *The Sopranos*. I couldn't get out of there fast enough!

"Excuse me," Stacey said meekly.

The gentlemen stared at us in a creepy kind of way; sort of like the way a lion in the zoo looks at that slab of meat before he tears into it with his teeth.

"What's your name, sweetheart?" the smaller of the two asked me.

"Ashley," I responded, not knowing what else to do. My quivering tone gave away my building fear.

"No need to be afraid, Ashley. You pretty ladies better watch yourselves around *him*; he's the one who's bad news." He nodded in Jake's direction.

I didn't know if he was joking or serious, but Jake appeared to be biting his lip or maybe his tongue to keep from responding to the crude remark.

"Goodbye," Jake growled in our direction.

Finally, the men moved aside and let us out. We hauled ass back to Mom-Mom's car.

"Who the fuck do you think they were?" Stacey asked once we were safely inside the car.

"I have no fucking idea, but they were scary as hell. I almost peed my pants when they came in. I thought they were gonna pull shotguns from under those leather jackets and start blasting!"

"Ashley, you've been watching too much tv," Stacey teased as we pulled off in a hurry.

# ❧Chapter Three❧

On the ride back to Stacey's house, I couldn't stop thinking about the two men who showed up at Jake's. I grabbed the steering wheel so tightly to keep my hands from shaking that my skin started to change colors.

"I hope they weren't there to kill Jake! He looked scared as shit, didn't he?"

"Yeah, he did. I don't think they would've let us leave if they were gonna hurt him, especially since we saw their faces," Stacey reasoned.

"I guess you're right," I agreed as we pulled up in front of her house. "Did you know Jake had a gun on him?"

"Oh shit! No, I didn't. We were about to be in the middle of some Wild Wild West shit!"

"We're going to have to find a new supplier," I told her.

"Naw, Jake is cool. Besides, I don't know anyone else close by that we can cop from on short notice like we do with Jake," Stacey reasoned.

Not knowing what to say, I shrugged my shoulders. Jake did always have what we needed when we needed it, which was often. So, for the time being, I let it go. I guess my need for drugs outweighed my fear, at least for the moment.

I checked my watch. It was already 2:30 p.m. Shit, time was going by too damn fast, and I hadn't even had my fix yet. I needed to hurry up so I'd have a few minutes to chill over Stacey's place before I had to get back home.

I hadn't revealed anything to Dr. Schultz other than the fact that the asshole I call Dad molested me. Yet, I couldn't stop the flood of memories that came back after telling her. I mean, there wasn't a day that had gone by since the nightmares began that I hadn't relived it over and over again, but usually, it was the same dream. All of a sudden, new memories started popping up. It seemed as if opening up to her literally opened my memory bank. So, I needed that hit and another and another to help me push those demons back in the closet.

I grabbed my bag off the back seat and followed Stacey inside her house. We went upstairs to her junkie-ass room, locked the door in case one of her parents came home early, and dumped out the contents of the bag. My bag had a dime bag of weed and a forty-dollar hit of heroin—my drug of choice.

"Come to mama," Stacey said as she grabbed the little clear bag containing Percocet and began crushing two with her Access card, a card her monthly welfare benefits were placed on, benefits that she sold to get money to buy drugs.

Once the pills were transformed into a fine white powder on the broken piece of mirror, she leaned over and inhaled deeply. She was a pro at it and her nose was like a vacuum; not one speck of powder was left when she finished.

I didn't have time for any of the other stuff; I only wanted one thing.

"Where's your lighter?"

Stacey tossed a small black *Bic* lighter, and I caught it with one hand.

"I guess all those years of softball paid off, huh?" Stacey said, thinking on the same page as me.

"I guess," I mumbled, as a feeling of regret washed over me about giving up a possible promising career for some dumb-ass boy. Just thinking of Rich for that one moment brought more feelings of pain and suffering to the surface. It seemed to be the story of my life.

Quickly, I dumped a little of the powder on the piece of Reynolds Wrap aluminum foil I pulled from my purse. Stacey tossed me a cut-up straw, which I quickly put between my dry lips. The blue flame under the foil immediately turned the powder into a brown liquid. I inhaled deeply while turning the foil in a circular motion, making sure not to miss a drop. When I finished done, that foil was almost clean enough to place back on the cardboard roll. Immediately, the calming effect began. *I love this shit!*

Without any effort on my part, I fell back on Stacey's other bed pillow with my eyes closed.

"Ash, you remember that first night you did this shit?"

"Yeah, seems like yesterday," I whispered, my eyes still shut.

"That was fucked up what Dawn did, though. She should've told people. Someone could've died that night."

"I should've whooped her ass," I mumbled, then thought back to the night of my first heroin hit.

*"You coming to my party tonight, Ash?" Dawn called and asked.*

*"Hell yeah! I wouldn't miss that shit for nothing in the world. I heard your parties are life-altering."*

*"Life-altering, huh?" She laughed. "I never heard that one before. Anyway, I'll see you tonight," she said, then hung up.*

*When I got to her house, there were kids everywhere, some from school and some from her neighborhood I assumed. I walked through the front door and was immediately stopped by Tyrone, one of the boys in my biology class.*

*"What's up, Ash?" he said, hugging all up on me.*

*"Hey, Ty," I said, shoving him back with both hands. "What's up with the hugging? We don't get down like that." Trying not to hurt his feelings, I laughed.*

*"Oh, it's like that, huh? I bet after you've been up in here for awhile you'll be singing a different tune."*

*"Whatever."*

*"Mark my words," he said before walking away.*

*I continued inside and stopped dead in my tracks. It was like something out of a movie. Kids were getting high everywhere with both alcohol and drugs. I saw this girl, Trish from Algebra class, with a bottle turned up like she was drinking soda. The distance didn't allow me to see the label, but the liquor was brown, which meant it was probably pretty lethal.*

*Inching further into the house, the smell of marijuana met my nose full on, but not before the clouds of smoke blurred my vision once I walked into the family room.*

*"Come here, Ash."*

*I heard someone calling me, but couldn't make out who it was until I got closer.*

*"Brenda?" I asked, my eyes burning and a little blurry.*

*"Yeah, it's me," she said as she pulled me down on the floor next to her.*

*"What the fuck?" I responded in bewilderment.*

*"I know. I told you her parties were crazy. Did you see the shit she has in the other room?"*

*"What, the booze?"*

*"Naw, the table filled with goodies."*

*"Nope. What kind of goodies?" I inquired.*

*Grabbing my arm and pulling me up from the floor, Brenda dragged me out of the family room and into the formal dining room. The main table had an assortment of food: cold cut trays, mini hoagies, cheeses, pepperoni, salads, wingettes, and other finger foods. On the buffet behind the counter was where all the liquor was set up. No one was serving the drinks; I guess that's why people like Trish were walking around with an entire bottle to their mouths.*

*Brenda turned my attention to another table off in the corner that had people sitting around it, while others just grabbed what they wanted and moved on.*

*"Is that..."*

*"Drugs?" Brenda finished the sentence for me.*

*I shook my head while confirming that's what I meant. I couldn't believe it; on the table was pouches of weed, a variety of pills—labeled, of course, and pouches of powder that I assumed was cocaine.*

*I knew Dawn's family was loaded, but damn, this shit was crazy!*

*"Shall we?" Brenda asked, motioning for me to help myself to the drug of my choice.*

*"Why not?" I responded as I grabbed a variety of stuff, some for now and some for later.*

*Shit, it was free. So, I was definitely taking advantage. That meant less money out my pocket. My little job at the mall didn't pay that much and definitely wasn't enough to cover my growing habit.*

*The house was so crowded that Brenda and I ended up upstairs in the bathroom. She rolled a joint while I emptied the powder on a small hand mirror I found in one of the vanity drawers. Brenda sat on the toilet and lit the joint, taking a few deep puffs before passing it to me.*

*"I'm about to hit this coke," I told her, passing back the joint after one good puff.*

*Just before I was about to inhale one of the lines, Dawn knocked on the bathroom door.*

*After realizing who it was, Brenda and I told her to come in. She smiled when she entered and saw what we were up to.*

*"Too many people downstairs, huh?"*

*"Hell yeah. We decided to come up here. Hope you don't mind," I said.*

*"No, I don't give a fuck."*

*"I hope this is some good coke," I told her, then used a dollar bill to inhale the fine powder.*

*"Coke?" She laughed. "That's not Coke, Ash," Dawn replied as I did another line.*

*"What the fuck is it?" I asked, wiping the residue from my nose as I peered in the mirror on the medicine cabinet.*

*"It's heroin. Don't you see the 'H' on the label?"*

*"What!"*

*Sure enough, I turned the second pouch over and the clear label had an 'H' on it. Immediately, I began to panic. I'd never done heroin before. Whenever Dawn and I partied together, she always had weed, xanies, percs, and coke. When the fuck did she start doing heroin!*

*"Calm down, Ash," she kept saying as I splashed my face with cold water from the sink.*

*"Are you kidding me? I never did this shit before! I have to go home in a little while. How long is it going to take this shit to wear off?"*

*I freaked out to the point where I made myself sick. I pushed Brenda off the toilet, lifted the lid, and on bended knees, I began sticking my fingers down my throat. Since I hadn't eaten anything, all I did was gag. Nothing came up.*

*I pulled my cell phone from my pocket and called Stacey, who happened to be downstairs with her cousin Pete at the party. Once I told her where I was, she came up to the bathroom. I could tell immediately she had been sampling Dawn's party favors, as well. Her eyes were red and half-closed.*

*"What's wrong, Ash?" she asked when she finally noticed I was upset.*

*"I just did heroin!" I screamed, expecting her to get as pissed about it as I was.*

*"That shit is the best, right?"*

*"What? You mean to tell me you're doing this shit, too?" I asked, bewildered.*

*"Yep," she confirmed. "Don't worry. Relax. In a few minutes, the shit will have you feeling mellow as hell."*

*Dawn and Brenda nodded their heads in agreement. I took a few deep breaths and allowed my adrenaline to come down. Once I stopped panicking,*

*I actually began to chill out. Before I knew it, I opened the other bag and snorted that, too. Brenda and Stacey walked me downstairs and found a spot for me on one of the sofas. Tyrone, who I saw when I arrived earlier, was sitting in the spot next to me.*

*"Hey, Ash," he said, then puffed on a joint and sipped something from a plastic cup.*

*"Hey, Ty," I replied all sexy-like, moving a little closer to him.*

*He leaned in and whispered in my ear, "Oh, it's like that now?"*

*I just batted my eyelashes and placed a light kiss on his lips. I was about to pull back, but he pulled me in for a full French kiss, and I didn't object. The next thing I knew, he grabbed my hand and pulled me up off the couch.*

*We ended up right back in the bathroom where I had just freaked out a few minutes earlier. He lifted me up under my arms and placed me on the edge of the vanity. Then he slid his hands underneath my shirt and began massaging my breasts. Normally, I would've slapped the shit out of him, but the heroin had me in another state of mind. I liked what Tyrone was doing, so I didn't stop him.*

*For the first time, I noticed just how fly Tyrone really was. His slim build made the too big jeans he was sporting hang just underneath his ass, showing off his Bart Simpson boxers. The white tee must've been an extra small, because his muscles appeared a lot bigger than they actually were. The backwards baseball cap with the Phillies logo completed his b-boy look. Yeah, this shit really had me feeling him. So, when he began undressing me, I helped him. As we were getting it on, I turned my head and noticed my reflection in the mirror on the door to the linen closet. I didn't see poor Ashley whose daddy molested her; I actually saw the beautiful, five-foot-six brunette, with the feminine but muscular physique from all the years of playing sports, who captivated people with her doe-shaped eyes. This shit was magical and already I wanted more.*

*"I told you that you'd be singing a different tune,"* he said.

*Once we were done, he left me in the bathroom with my pants down around my ankles.*

*I helped myself to another freebie after I got myself together and made it back downstairs. I looked at Tyrone and smiled. He will never know about the tears I cried when he left me in that bathroom feeling like shit. I pretended his comment and abrupt departure didn't faze me one bit. After all, he wasn't the first to take advantage of me and probably wouldn't be the last.*

*I went in search of a ride home; I'd had enough of fake friends for one night.*

*By the time Stacey and her cousin dropped me home, I wasn't pissed with Dawn anymore. I actually felt more relaxed than I had in a long time. All the shit I had been going through didn't seem to matter at the moment. That was what I wanted whenever I got high, but the weed and pills just didn't give me the same effect that I got from the heroin that night.*

*When I found out from Dawn that a hit of heroin costs the same as a dime bag of weed—that I could buy a ten- or twenty-dollar hit—I was hooked. That was about six months ago, and I've been using ever since.*

My trip down memory lane ended abruptly a few moments later.

"Stacey! What the hell is going on in here?"

Stacey and I opened our eyes to her mother standing in the doorway with her hands on her hips.

There were drugs all over the bed. I was scared shitless, but Stacey didn't seem fazed.

"Oh shit! I thought you locked the door! I gotta go," I said, grabbing my things and running past Stacey's mom.

"I gotta fix that fucking lock," I heard Stacey mumble on my way out.

"Come back here, Ashley Kennedy," her mom called after me.

"I'm sorry, but I really have to go," I yelled back as I pulled the front door open and slammed it shut behind me.

It took my shaky hands a few times before I got the key in the ignition. I don't know how I made it home, but I did in one piece. Pop-Pop was parked in the driveway, so I had to park on the street instead. Parallel parking wasn't my thing, and on top of that, I backed into the next-door neighbor's car.

"Shit!" I said, while quickly inspecting the car for damage.

Now I had to worry about Stacey's mom calling to tell on me *and* Ms. Clarke next door finding out I backed into her car and put a little crack in her front grill. *Why does this shit always happen to me?*

"Ashley," Mom-Mom called out as soon as I stumbled through the door.

I tried to sneak in, but that annoying creek in the door gave me away once again.

"Gotta pee," I said, trying to sound as normal as possible while hurrying upstairs away from her view.

If she had gotten a good look at me, I didn't know what she would do. Thankfully, I heard her car start up and saw her pull away from my window.

Flopping down on my bed, I tried to get back the feeling I had before Stacey's mom came into her room. Sadly, the only way to do that was to dig into the stash I got at Jake's and take another hit. Doing six bags a day started getting expensive.

*I'm gonna have to start doing overtime at my dumb-ass job just to get more money. I may even need a second job,* I thought.

Unlike Stacey, I double-checked that my door was locked before preparing another hit. Locking my door had been a habit for years, even though I knew I was safe in my home. I guess it gave me a sense of security.

Quickly, I pulled out the little black mirror that was missing its handle from the drawer of my nightstand and placed it on top of the magazines lying there. I dumped the contents from the ten-dollar bag onto it. Then I sat down on the floor cross-legged with my back against the side of the bed and brought the mirror eye level. I compressed my nostril with a fingertip and inhaled the powder quickly before someone popped up.

Once I was done, I unlocked the door and fell back on my comfy queen-size bed. I tried to find my happy place—the place where everything was wonderful and the demons couldn't find me. It wasn't working.

# ❧Chapter Four❧

Aunt Chris and I were back at Dr. Schultz's office for my third session. It took her two weeks to convince me to return after the first one. After revealing a little of the specifics about my dad at the second session, I couldn't stop crying for a week. Every night that week, I experienced the "monster in the closet" dreams, something I hadn't had in a long time.

Now that Dr. Schultz had a clearer understanding of the situation, she urged me to include my mom in what was going on.

"Ashley has something to tell you," Dr. Schultz began.

I looked everywhere but at my mom. *I can't do this to her; she will never be the same*, I thought, then looked over at Aunt Chris for help.

"Marie—" Aunt Chris began.

Dr. Schultz raised her hand to stop her in mid-sentence.

"Chris, I really feel it's best if Ashley tells her mother. I know she's scared, but she can't keep using you as a crutch or shield. She will not begin to deal with this until she can tell people herself and not feel ashamed or responsible."

"What's going on? What does she need to feel ashamed or responsible for?" Mom asked, clearly confused. "I thought Chris was bringing her here because she was stressed about school and stuff."

"Ashley...," Aunt Chris spoke my name and gave me a look that asked if I was ready to take that step.

I went from biting my once-beautiful nails down to the meat to wringing my hands nervously as I tried to keep them from shaking uncontrollably. As I began speaking, the shake in my voice matched that of my hands. It would've been the perfect time to run out and take a hit to calm all the emotions that were running rampant inside of me. Unfortunately, I couldn't. So, with a very deep breath to calm me, I finally uttered the words.

"Mom, I..." I hesitated.

"Go ahead, Ashley. You can do it," Dr. Schultz encouraged.

"Mom, I was molested."

Before I could say more, my mom had already gotten out of her seat and was headed in my direction with tears streaming down her face.

"Who...who did this to you, Ashley?" she questioned.

As she embraced me, the words disappeared within the strands of my long, straight hair. I hugged her tightly and said the dreaded words that would tear her world apart, just as it had mine for all these years.

"Daddy," I told her, sounding like that five-year-old child once again.

With that one word, she fell apart right there in front of my eyes.

"No! No! No!" she screamed repeatedly.

Immediately, I was on the floor where she had fallen in agony. I tried to comfort her broken heart, but it was useless.

"It's okay, Mommy. It's not your fault," I kept trying to tell her.

She couldn't believe she was an unknowing accomplice to this crime against her child. It took forever to bring her tears to a halt. I handed her a few of the tissues that always seemed to be in my jacket pocket. She finally got herself together, and by the time we left Dr. Schultz's office, the three of us looked like we'd been on a drinking binge for days. Our eyes were so red and puffy.

The moment we left the doctor's office, my mom called my dad's mom.

"Theresa, my daughter just told me that your fucking low-down, dirty son molested her!"

I didn't hear my grandmother's response, but I can only guess it was not what my mother wanted to hear.

"Oh, so you think Ashley would lie about something like this? Really! Well, let me clue you in on something. By the time I'm done talking with the police and my lawyers, you will be visiting your scumbag of a son in jail or the cemetery! He will not spend another day on this earth unscathed by his acts of malice towards his own flesh and blood!"

She almost broke her phone as she ended the call. The phone hit the ground; her hands were shaking so badly.

"I can't believe this motherfucker just came to her birthday party like nothing happened," my mom continued to rant during the ride home.

"You were wondering why her whole demeanor changed when he showed up with his mother and the boys. Now you know," Aunt Chris told her.

"When did you find out?" Mom asked Aunt Chris.

"That night after she and Mom got into that big blow-out over her leaving the party early. She came to my house, and I took her to the mall to clear her head so she and Mommy could talk calmly. After we did some shopping, like we always do when one of us is upset, I took her back. She kept saying how much she wished she never knew who her dad was, and I couldn't understand why. After I kept probing, she finally decided to tell me why. I never expected to hear what came out of her mouth."

"Ashley, why didn't you tell me?" my mom asked with apparent hurt in her tone.

"I'm sorry. I just couldn't. I didn't want you to blame yourself for what happened."

"You could've told me back then. I would've had his ass in jail so fast his head would still be spinning. Why didn't you say anything, Ash?"

"I was afraid. I thought people would say it was my fault or say I was lying...I don't know," I said, then dropped my head in my hands.

I needed to get out of that car and get a hit...fast. My chest felt so tight that I thought I was having a heart attack. For the remainder of the ride home, I shut down and let Mom and Aunt Chris discuss me like I wasn't even there. I lay across the back seat of Aunt Chris's Accord and stared up at the evening stars as they whizzed by. My emotional state allowed the past to creep into my thoughts.

*"I love my new princess bed, Daddy. It matches everything in my room. The princess chair, the light on my dresser, and the big poster on my wall of Sleeping Beauty and Cinderella," I told him excitedly when I arrived earlier that day for my weekend visit.*

*"I'm glad, baby," he told me, then kissed me on the forehead before heading downstairs to the group of friends that always seemed to be there whenever I visited.*

*My little brothers were away, so I decided to stay in my room and play with my toys. The princess canopy had a little door for me to climb inside and play with my dolls where no one could see me.*

*My Barbies were having a party and dancing to the music coming through the vent from the party Daddy was having downstairs. I was having so much fun and the music was so loud that I didn't even hear him come in until he called out to me.*

*"Ashley baby, come to Daddy," my father said with his arms outstretched, welcoming me.*

*My five-year-old mind ate up the affection my daddy was showing at the moment. He was usually too busy with his friends or my little brothers and their mother.*

*"Here I come, Daddy," I said, dropping my dolls and climbing out of the canopy.*

*I jumped onto his lap as he sat on the edge of my bed. He rubbed my hair affectionately, like people do dogs, and planted sloppy kisses on my face.*

*"Stop, Daddy," I giggled, while lovingly looking up into his face.*

*Daddy had some white powder all over his nose. It looked like the powder from the donuts I love.*

*"What's that stuff on your face, Daddy? Did you have a powdered donut? Did you get one for me?"*

When I took my little finger and tried to wipe some of it off his nose, Daddy got really mad and slapped my hand away. I began to cry.

"I'm sorry. You know Daddy loves you, right?" his voice echoed in my ear as he pulled me close and wiped away the tears that trickled down my face.

Immediately, I stopped crying and nodded as a huge smile spread across my face. I wrapped my tiny arms around his neck and hugged him tightly.

"I'm sorry, Daddy. I just want to taste the powder, too," I told him.

"I'll get you one next time," he lied, patting my back while I continued to cling to him.

An innocent father-daughter moment quickly changed to a weird scene from a movie. Daddy's rough hand felt like sandpaper against my legs as he rubbed them, gliding higher and higher up my thigh with each stroke. His long fingers pulled at the elastic of my tiny pink floral panties underneath my yellow sundress that he had pushed up around my waist.

"Daddy, what are you doing?" I asked, while trying to pull my dress down and squirm out of his grasp.

*He was holding me too tightly around my waist. I could barely move. It felt like he was crushing me. I began to panic.*

*"Let go, Daddy!" I screamed in his ear, while punching him with my tiny fists.*

*"Daddy loves you, baby girl. Why are you fighting Daddy? I'm just trying to give you a kiss," he said, forcing my lips to meet his.*

*"Get off of me! Get off of me!"*

*Without any warning, he flipped me and dropped me down on the bed. I was now partially inside the canopy that I'd been playing in moments before. He couldn't see my face, so he didn't notice the terrified expression or the tears that were falling on the Barbie clothes I was lying on top of. Nothing but the lower half of my body was exposed to his blurred vision.*

*He grabbed my flailing legs and pulled them apart as I tried to kick him anywhere that would hopefully stop his assault. No matter how loud I screamed he didn't stop his probing. The music downstairs blared, and the people down there were in their own drug- and alcohol-induced stupor. So, my cries that I'm sure could be heard through the vent, if anyone cared to listen, fell on deaf ears. What I heard above my own screams was the ripping of the fabric of my pretty panties...*

"Stop! Get off of me!" I cried out.

"Ash! Ashley! Wake up, baby!" my mom screamed as she tried to shake me awake.

I jumped up and looked around. I had fallen asleep in the back of Aunt Chris' car. Looking out the window, I realized we were parked in front of Mom-Mom and Pop-Pop's house.

"Ash, do you remember what Dr. Schultz said before we left her office?" Aunt Chris asked.

"What?" I was too stressed at the moment to remember anything other than the nightmare I'd just had.

"She said her office is obligated to report the situation to child services."

"So..." I responded.

"So we have to tell Mom-Mom and Pop-Pop before someone shows up here to investigate the allegations," my mom informed me.

"Oh hell no! I'm not telling anyone else! I wish I never told you two!" I yelled, then jumped out the car before either of them could respond.

I pulled out my door key, let myself in, and ran straight upstairs to my room. After closing and locking the door behind me, I headed for my stash.

"Damn, I only got two bags left!"

I didn't bother being neat and precise about it; I dumped the contents of one of the bags onto my trusty mirror and snorted it up before someone came knocking at my door. I looked in the mirror and checked to make sure there was no evidence on my face. Then I stuck the tip of my finger in my mouth and moistened it before sliding it across the mirror. Once I collected the leftover residue, I put my finger in my mouth and sucked it clean.

*What the fuck have I gotten myself into? I should've kept this shit to myself. Now the whole fucking family has to know!*

I flopped down on my bed and buried my head in my pillow where my screams couldn't be heard. How was I going to tell Mom-Mom and Pop-Pop? I just didn't know how much more I could handle. When was this nightmare going to end?

# ❧Chapter Five❧

My third counseling session really tripped my out. So, I took a much-needed trip over to Dawn's house. Since it was still early in the afternoon, I had all day to hang out over there and get cozy with my powder friend...or at least that's what I thought. Mom-mom's call interrupted my high.

"Ashley," she said as soon as I picked up.

"Yes, Mom-Mom."

"I need you to come home immediately," she told me, sounding like she was crying.

"What's wrong?" I asked with concern.

"There are some people here from Child Services. I don't understand what they're talking about, Ashley. I need you to come home."

"What?"

My mind immediately went back to Dr. Schultz's office. After our session with Dr. Schultz, I thought I'd have a few days to work up to telling them about what my dad did, but that wasn't the case. Her office was obligated to tell Child Services immediately after being told of the sexual abuse. She did hold off until the session with my mom, but immediately afterwards, she made the notification.

"Okay," I agreed and hit the end button before throwing the phone on Dawn's bed.

"What's wrong, Ash?" Dawn wanted to know.

"I can't talk about it. I got to go. Do you have more? I need another hit bad."

"Sure. I'm getting more later. Take some," Dawn urged.

When my cell rang again, I knew I didn't have time to do another hit. I hoped what I had done already would help get me through the ambush I was about to walking into.

I picked up a twenty-dollar bag from Dawn's stash and handed her the ten dollars I had on me, with a promise to give her the rest later.

I left Dawn's and walked down the street to the Marshall Road stop. I looked down the tracks in the direction of home just in time to see the end of the trolley round the bend ahead. I plopped down on the steel green bench bolted into the ground for waiting passengers. Leaning forward, I dropped my head into my hands and thought about what awaited me.

*It's cool, Ash. It's not your fault; it's on him*, I tried to convince myself.

The next trolley arrived ten minutes later. *Why couldn't it break down so I could have an excuse as to why I can't make it?* Six minutes later, I paid my fare and stepped off the trolley. I really wanted to just keep riding until the operator forced me to get off. I wanted to go anywhere but home. Unfortunately, I had no choice.

Opening the door, I stepped into another chapter of my living hell. I was surprised to see my mom and Aunt Chris there, as well. I thought they were at work.

"I called them," Mom-Mom said, as if reading my mind.

Aunt Chris, who was standing close to the door, whispered, "Stay calm."

"Can you tell me why the hell I have people from Child Protective Services in my damn house questioning me and your grandmother like we're criminals? Walking around here inspecting my damn house; this is some bullshit!" Pop-Pop expressed with obvious displeasure.

"Again, Mr. Kennedy, we're terribly sorry about all this. We had no idea you and your wife hadn't been informed of what transpired," said the man in the *Men in Black* suit.

"No, we weren't," Pop-Pop responded while looking directly at me.

I was still standing near the door with my mouth hanging open.

"Sit down, Ashley," Pop-Pop said, anger evident in his tone.

"Hello, Ashley. I'm Ms. Chancellor and this is Mr. Tyler. We're from Delaware County Child Services. We'd like to talk to you about some information we received from your therapist, Dr. Schultz."

I slid into the single chair opposite the sofa and love seat that everyone else was occupying, except Pop-Pop who remained standing.

I was feeling relaxed from my recent activity at Dawn's, and my slouched posture in the chair, although involuntary, was immediately noticed by Pop-Pop.

"Sit up," he commanded.

I did as he said and tried to concentrate. I just wanted to get this over with, so I could go up to my room and take the hit I had in my pocket.

"Ashley, you shared some information with Dr. Schultz, and our office needs to investigate your accusations," stated Ms. Chancellor.

"What accusations?" Pop-Pop wanted to know.

Knowing I didn't want to talk about it, my mom jumped in and handled the situation for me.

"Dad, Johnny molested Ashley," she said, not bothering to beat around the bush.

"Bullshit! Molested her when? Until her birthday a few weeks ago, she hasn't seen the man in years," he argued.

"When she was little, Dad, and spending the weekends with him," Aunt Chris jumped in.

Mom-Mom remained silent. She was as still as a statue, except for her hands that I noticed were shaking uncontrollably.

"Ashley, Mr. Tyler needs to ask you some specific questions," Ms. Chancellor informed me.

My insides immediately began churning, and I felt like the McDonald's Big Mac and fries I had at Dawn's was about to rise up and spill all over the oriental rug beneath my feet.

"Excuse me," I said as I jumped up and ran upstairs to the bathroom.

I threw the toilet seat up, fell to my knees as I leaned over, and vomited my lunch. After a few minutes, I wiped my mouth with the back of my hand before sitting back and placing my head against the tub behind me. The coldness from the tub felt good on my neck. After a few more minutes, I got up and walked over to the sink, where I washed my face, hands, and brushed my teeth.

"As soon as this is over, I'm definitely doing this bag I just got from Dawn," I told myself as I patted my pocket, expecting to feel the bag of powder inside.

"Shit!" I patted my pocket again and then dug inside searching for the bag I placed there before leaving Dawn's. It wasn't there, and I began freaking out. I pulled my pants down, checking to see if maybe I had a hole in my pocket and somehow the little baggie fell inside my pant leg. Frantically, I damn near undressed searching for that bag before I heard my mom coming up the steps.

"Ash," my mom called out as she turned the knob that I forgot to lock and entered the bathroom.

She looked at me in my state of near nakedness with a confused expression on her face.

"What happened?" she asked.

"I got sick from the food I ate earlier."

"Did you get it on your clothes?"

"I thought I did," I told her as I began putting my clothes back on.

"Come on down so you can talk to this man and they can go before Pop-Pop loses his composure."

"I'll be right there as soon as I brush my teeth," I lied.

I needed a few minutes to look around on the floor for my shit. As soon as she closed the door, I dropped down and searched around the tub and the toilet. No bag. Heading downstairs, I now dreaded two things: talking to this man about what my sick-ass daddy did and someone finding my little bag of magic powder.

As I reached the bottom of the steps, prepared to return to the chair I occupied a few minutes ago, Pop-Pop sat in it. *Shit! How am I going to check the chair for my little bag of powder now that he's in it?* I stood awkwardly at the bottom of the steps, not sure what to do.

"Ashley, you and Mr. Tyler can go in the kitchen and talk," Mom said, interrupting my thoughts.

"Okay," I replied.

I didn't want to talk to Mr. Tyler or anyone else; I wanted my shit! As I turned around before entering the kitchen, I saw Pop-Pop get out of the chair. I was ready to run over there and dig around the cushion, but Mr. Tyler broke into my thoughts of escape.

"Ashley, this shouldn't take very long," he said, while pulling out one of the kitchen chairs and offering it to me. He seemed to be a nice guy, and I knew he was there to help me, but what I wanted at the moment he couldn't do a damn thing about!

We sat at the table for what seemed like hours while he asked me questions about dickhead Johnny and the fucked-up shit he did to me.

"Ashley, I know this is difficult, but just try to answer the questions as best as you can. Okay?"

"Okay," I answered, resigning myself to the fact that there was no way out.

I told him the basic stuff, but not the deep-down dirty shit; he didn't need to know that. Truthfully, no one did.

"Can you tell me who harmed you?"

"My dad."

"Can you state his name for the record?"

"Johnny Wynton."

"At the time that these alleged allegations occurred, was there anyone else around?"

*A whole house full of fucking people* is what I wanted to say, but I didn't.

"Yes, at times there was."

"Can you tell me who?"

"His girlfriend, Angie, and usually some of the people he got high with. I don't really remember their names."

"Did any of them know what was going on?"

"Yes. A few of them participated."

"Excuse me," he stuttered, not expecting that answer.

"Sometimes he included other people."

"Can you be more specific?"

"He liked to watch as much as he liked to do it himself."

"Was his girlfriend a participant?"

"No, but I know she knew what was going on. When I told her what he was doing to me...she called me a liar," I said, feeling as dejected as I did the day it happened.

If I couldn't get her to believe me and she was right there, I knew no one else would. That day, I vowed to never tell another soul and to never return to that house of horrors again.

As the questions continued, my answers came out very monotone. It was like I had no emotions at all. Truthfully, every question brought the bile in my stomach closer to the surface. If he didn't stop soon, I felt I would surely vomit right at the kitchen table.

Finally, he got what he came for and they left. After repeating some of the questions to Mom, Aunt Chris, and Mom-Mom, they went out on the deck where Pop-Pop was sitting smoking cigarette after cigarette. Finally, I was able to go in search of my shit.

"Yes!" I whispered when I found it right on the side of the plastic-covered chair cushion. I was so happy I actually kissed it. I went right upstairs, ready to open that bad boy up and sniff away.

The sound of my mom screaming diverted my attention. I walked back to the top of the stairs where I could hear her even clearer.

"Tell that to the judge!" my mom screamed into the receiver when my grandmother finished her tirade.

"Calm down, Marie, please," Mom-Mom said quietly.

"That bitch just pissed me off!"

"What did she say, Marie?"

"She had the nerve to ask me how dare Ashley hurl these accusations at her son! Talking about he's been nothing but a great father to all his kids. Is she seriously calling that drugged-out fool a good dad?"

"I take it the police or Child Services showed up at his house, too."

"I guess so. I hope they took his ass straight to jail!" Mom screamed.

I slowly maneuvered down the steps and saw Mom-mom consoling my mom.

"Ashley, can you come outside, please?" she asked when she looked up at me.

My mother just shook her head and walked out to the patio alone.

"Please tell Pop-Pop what's going on. He's having a hard time believing what you're saying about Johnny," Mom-Mom finished.

I nodded my head as I made my way down the rest of the steps. I didn't feel comfortable having this conversation with Pop-Pop: one, because it was embarrassing, and two, because I already knew he didn't believe me. I told him the same stuff I told Mr. Tyler. Well, most of it. Yet, he still seemed unsure of my innocence. I guess unlike Pop-Pop, Child Services believed me enough to pay dear old Dad a visit since my grandmother had called talking shit.

A few days passed, and now it was in the hands of the court. Ever since Child Services showed up, Mom-Mom seemed to age ten years. I couldn't tell if the puffiness under her eyes was from lack of sleep or all the crying she'd been doing.

I knew it wasn't over, but for the moment, I pretended it was. I imagined Johnny was in jail being raped repeatedly by guys that looked like the ones that showed up at Jake's the other day. That brought a smile to my face, the first smile associated with Johnny in a long time.

I went back to drawing a picture of Timmy, who lay on the sofa across from where I sat at the dining room table. He and I had been at the neighborhood playground for almost two hours, and now he was sound asleep. *What I wouldn't give to be a two-year-old again.*

I wished I could find something besides fucking drugs to help me finally get a good night's sleep. Really, when I thought about it, even they didn't help me sleep. Most nights, I stayed up writing in my journal or drawing, two things I was good at. I couldn't remember the last time I actually slept through the night. I guess the saying *"I'll sleep when I'm dead"* is true.

# ❧Chapter Six❧

"Hey, Mia," I said when my best friend since first grade answered the phone.

"Hey, Ash. What's up with you?"

"Not a damn thing," I told her, while lying across the bed on my stomach with my legs dangling off the edge. "You want to hang out today? I was thinking about hitting the mall with Dawn and Brenda."

"Sorry, Ash, I can't. I have plans already."

"Oh, it's cool. I just wanted to see if you were free," I said, feeling rejected.

"Maybe another time?"

"Alright," I agreed before disconnecting the call.

Immediately, I felt some type of way. Ever since Mia found out I was getting high with Stacey, Brenda, and Dawn, she seemed to pull away.

*"I can't stand them, Ash,"* she told me one day after hanging out with us.

I knew she didn't get high or do anything bad at all, for that matter, but I didn't expect her to start acting the way she did.

*"They're cool, Mia. They just like to get high and have fun,"* I replied, trying to reason with her.

*"I'm sorry, but that's not my thing. If you want to hang out with them, be my guest,"* she said before walking away.

After that day, our friendship changed drastically. Whenever she saw me at school with one of them, she would wave, maybe stop and talk for a few minutes, but that was it. She wanted no parts of them or me when I was with them. That really hurt me because it had always been Ashley and Mia. We did everything together. My house was her home away from home, and it was the same for me at hers. The fact that she turned her back on me, at least in my eyes, added to the internal struggle I already had going on.

Once Mia became more distant, I gravitated towards my new friends even more. My friendship with the new "it" girls had me doing all kinds of shit I never would've done when it was just Mia and I.

This latest rejection opened an old wound, and like always, drugs were my band-aid. I didn't feel like going to the mall anymore. I wanted to get high. I didn't have any more heroin, but I had a couple Xanax that Stacey traded me for some weed I had the other night. I popped one and then prepared to go over Stacey's, until I remembered the last time I was there and her mother walked in on us.

"Where's your mom?" I asked when I called to see if the coast was clear.

"She's working a double, so she won't be home 'til tomorrow."

"What about your pop?"

"He's on the road; won't be back until next week. Life of a trucker..."

"Cool. I'll be over in a few. You get the shit from Jake?"

"Yeah. You better stop being a scaredy cat and take your ass back over there."

"Fuck that. Did you see the Mob guys?"

"No, Ashley," she laughed.

"It's not funny, Stacey. I'll be there in a few."

Grabbing my cell phone, I pulled up the SEPTA app to see what time the next trolley was due. The schedule said three-fifteen, which would be in ten minutes. I straightened up the covers on my bed, threw the clothes that were all over the floor into the closet, and shut it. I'd clean it up when I got back.

"Mom-Mom, I'm about to catch the trolley over Stacey's for awhile!" I yelled so she could hear me in the kitchen.

"Alright. Don't stay too long, Ashley. Be back in time for dinner."

"Okay."

I made it around the corner just as the trolley rounded the bend. After dropping my fare in the machine, I walked to the back where there were a few empty seats. School had just let out, and the trolley was packed with rowdy high school kids, a few that I knew.

As soon as I sat down, I began to feel the effect of the pill I just popped. I did my best to stay alert so I wouldn't miss my stop. If it weren't for a kid named Stevie talking shit, I probably would have nodded off.

"What's up, Ash?"

"Nothing, Stevie," I mumbled.

"I haven't seen you in awhile."

"I've been around," I said, although I really didn't feel like talking. I just wanted to enjoy the chill mode I was in from the Xanie.

He inched a little closer to my ear and whispered, "My boy Ty said you got the bomb shit."

"Who? What?" I asked, confused.

"Ty, Tyrone...the one you let hit that a while back in Dawn's bathroom."

"Get the fuck out of my face, Stevie!" I shoved him away from me.

"Damn, Ash, don't get mad. It was a compliment. I was about to ask if I can get a taste," he stated with a laugh.

"No, but you can get my fucking fist in your mouth if you don't leave me alone! And tell Tyrone I hope he enjoyed it, 'cause he won't get it again!"

"That's not what he said. He told me all he got to do is break you off with some of that shit and he can get whatever he wants from you," he responded loud enough for others to hear and turn in my direction.

"Fuck you, Stevie!" I screamed as tears began to fall.

I pushed past him to the back door. In my anger and haste, I got off a stop too soon. Wile walking the extra three blocks to Stacey's, I was pissed. Tears continued falling as I thought about Stevie's crude comment. It wasn't so much what he said. It's just that guys had been abusing me for as long as I could remember, and mostly because I let them.

Thoughts of Mike and Rich, two ex-boyfriends who were both links in the chain of abuse that surrounded me, came to mind, and I couldn't get to Stacey's fast enough.

As soon as she opened the door to my tear-stained face, she knew what I needed.

"What's wrong?" she asked as we walked up to her room.

"It'd be easier to tell you what's right, which isn't much these days either."

As we chilled in her room getting high, I told her what Stevie said. Forgeting about the pill I took before leaving home, I began snorting the bags of heroin she had picked up from Jake's for me. I did one as soon as I got there, followed by another less than an hour later, even though the Xanax already had me in chill mode...or at least I was before Stevie's bullshit. Stacey was high, too; so, she had no idea how much I'd done.

"Ashley! Ashley!" Stacey kept screaming.

"Huh?" I answered.

"Ash!" she screamed again as I began to nod off once more.

She began shaking me vigorously. The combination of the Xanax and heroin was a lethal cocktail. My heart and respiration had slowed down so much that Stacey began to panic. While sitting in the deep-cushioned chair in her room, my head kept falling forward, as I was in what they call a nod. You know how when you fall asleep sitting up and your head drops, then snaps back quickly? Well, mine wasn't snapping back, and Stacey started freaking out.

"Ash," she began to cry.

I heard her voice calling me, but she sounded so far away. In reality, she was right next to me. I tried to open my eyes, but they just wouldn't cooperate.

My cell phone started going off. Stacey really freaked out when she saw Mom-Mom's name on the screen.

"Ash! Your grandmom is on the phone! Get up, Ash," she begged.

Not knowing what else to do when Mom-Mom hung up and called right back, Stacey answered the phone.

"Hi, Ms. Nicolette," I heard her say. "She's in the bathroom. She wasn't feeling well ... Yes, I'll tell her ... Okay, goodbye," Stacey said before turning to me again after hanging up. "You're late for dinner, Ash! You know how your grandmom is about being home on time."

"I know," I replied drowsily as I began coming around.

Stacey left the room and returned with a cold rag, which she placed on my face in an attempt to get me coherent. She repeated this process for a good ten minutes. Once she saw a little improvement, she called her cousin Pete to come give me a ride home. There was no way she would let me take the trolley. Hell, I probably wouldn't have made it to the trolley stop, especially since I couldn't even feel my legs.

She and Pete had to help me downstairs and into his car for the short ride home. Despite still being fucked up, when Stacey asked me if I wanted my other bag of magic powder that was on the floor by my feet, I didn't hesitate to tell her yes.

She stuffed it in my backpack when she pulled out my keys and opened the door for me.

"Can you make it, Ash?" Stacey whispered in my ear.

"Yeah, I'm cool," I said and took my keys from her, stuffing them in my pocket.

She made a quick exit when she heard everyone in the kitchen. Thank God Pop-Pop had finally oiled that noisy-ass screen door. I crawled upstairs thankfully unnoticed. I threw my keys on the nightstand and my backpack on the floor before falling onto my bed.

"Ashley! Ashley!"

I opened my eyes and saw Mom-Mom standing there.

"When did you come in? Why didn't you come eat?" she asked, bending over and picking up my backpack from the floor.

"I been here," I told her, having no real perception of time. I just assumed I'd been asleep for a while since my high had worn off enough for me to hold a conversation.

"Are you sick? Your eyes look funny."

"No, I'm just tired. I ate something at Stacey's," I lied.

"Ashley, you know how I feel about dinner. Do something with this," she said, then tossed the bag in my direction.

I sat up and snatched it as it sailed my way. The zipper was partially open, and when I caught it, it flipped and spilled some of my stuff out.

"What's all that?" she asked as a few of the backpack's contents sprawled out on my bed.

As she reached for my spiral notebook, I hollered, "No!"

"What's wrong with you?" She pulled her hand back like I had slapped it.

"Nothing. That's my private thoughts in there. I don't want anyone to read them," I explained.

She looked at me strangely, but accepted my explanation.

"Don't you have to work tomorrow?" Mom-Mom asked.

"Yeah," I responded, instantly thinking about how much I hated my job. The only perk was the discount on the clothes...and my little hookup.

"Do you need a ride?"

"Yeah."

"Stop saying yeah. You know how much I hate that. The word is yes."

"Yes, Mom-Mom."

"What time are you in?"

"Nine forty-five."

"Alright. Clean that mess up," she said, waving her hand in the direction of the items on my bed. She then left, closing the door behind her.

Immediately, I reached over and locked it. Next, I grabbed the notebook and pulled the small plastic pouch from the spiral ring, careful not to tear it. My eyes zoned in on it as soon as I looked at the book when it hit my flowered comforter. I didn't remember how it got in my bag.

I picked up my cell phone from the bed and called Stacey.

"Stacey, what the fuck happened?" I whispered when she answered.

"Ash! Oh my God, girl. What the fuck did you take before you got here?"

I paused for a moment to think. That's when I remembered the pill.

"Xanax."

"Girl, I thought I was gonna have to call an ambulance. You were fucked up! I thought you stopped breathing a couple times. You scared the shit out of me," she said, continuing her tirade.

"Sorry, Stace. I don't know what I was thinking."

"You were so upset about dumb-ass Stevie," she reminded me.

"Oh yeah, I almost forgot about that," I mumbled as the earlier conversation came back to mind.

"You coming over tomorrow?"

"Maybe later in the day. I work from ten to six."

"Alright. I may come up there and cop a few things," she informed me.

She was referring to our little hookup at my job.

"I'll text you and let you know who I'm working with. If it's TJ, you can come. He doesn't care what happens in that store as long as he gets a cut."

"Okay, well, let me know. I'm about to crash for the night."

"Cool. I'll hit you up tomorrow when I get there."

I was about to hang up when I remembered the bag of powder.

"Stace, did you put the bag of powder in my backpack?"

"Yeah, I did. It was on the floor, and I asked you if you wanted it for later. You said yeah, so I dropped it in there. Why? Did something happen to it?" she asked, concerned.

"No, but Mom-Mom almost saw it."

"Oh shit! You've been having close calls all day, girl. You better chill for the rest of the night."

"Yeah, you might be right. Talk to you tomorrow."

"Later," she said and hung up.

I dropped the phone back on the bed and began cleaning up the stuff that fell out of my bag. Just as I was about to close my notebook, the title of one of the poems I had written caught my eye. I'd written it that first night after I got high at Dawn's. Even though I was high then, my mind seemed clearer than ever before...

*Mistake*

*Today I lie here in this bed*

*Thinking of all the things you said*

*You told me, "No matter what you have to go through,*

*I will always be there for you"*

*Well, Daddy, you lied to me*
*I need you more now*
*And you're nowhere to be found*
*When I was little, I would look up in the stands*
*and search for your face*
*Most of the time, you weren't there; someone else*
*was in your place*
*Once in a while, you would be there*
*I'd see you and think you did care*
*But, then, you hurt me*
*And your face was not the one I wanted to see*
*Instead, I looked for the faces of those that really*
*do care*
*The ones I know will always be there*
*You have two boys now to care for*
*I pray you don't treat them the way you treated me*
*As a mistake...*

Tears fall from my eyes and wet the page, smudging the words that were as truthful as I could be. Quickly, I grabbed my light blue towel off the hook on the back of my door and headed to the bathroom for a quick shower. It had been a long-ass day full of shit that continued to weigh me down. Thinking about what Stacey said, I realized I almost fucked up. Taking that pill and then snorting all that powder almost sent my ass to the hospital, or maybe the morgue.

*Is that where I'll end up if I don't stop?* Sadly, the thought didn't faze me enough to make me stop.

I turned on the shower, adjusted the water to steamy hot, and stepped in.

My night ended like it always did, with a quick hit. Except this time, I did a lot less.

*After the day I've had, I shouldn't tempt fate.*

# ❧Chapter Seven❧

"Let's go, Ashley. You're going to be late," Mom-Mom yelled from the bottom of the steps.

"I'm coming," I yelled back.

I took one final look in the mirror to make sure there was no evidence from my quick fix showing. I grabbed my backpack and some tissues from the box on my nightstand for my runny nose.

"You catching another cold?" Mom-Mom asked when she saw me wiping my nose.

"Yeah," I lied.

"I'm going to have to take you to the doctor. You've been catching colds quite frequently lately. Every time I see you, you have a tissue to your nose. Maybe it's allergies," she said, her voice full of concern. "Where'd that come from?"

She pointed to a red, bumpy rash on my arm that I'd been scratching. It was a fiery red color and stood out like a bloody nose against my pale skin.

"I'm not sure. Maybe it's the detergent," I lied again.

"The detergent? Ashley, I've been using the same detergent forever. How are you allergic to it all of a sudden?" she asked, clearly confused.

The truth was, I didn't know where it came from, but I met one of Brenda's friends who had a bad one on both arms and her back. She told me it was a side effect from doing a combination of drugs, especially the pills.

I shrugged my shoulders when I noticed Mom-Mom still looking at me with a puzzled expression on her face.

The fifteen-minute car ride to work was an unusually silent one. I peeked over at her, and she looked lost in thought.

"You okay, Mom-Mom?"

"Yes. I'm just concerned, Ashley. So much is going on with you these days. This stuff with your father, maybe it's taking a toll on you physically now

box 84 box

that you're talking about. These constant colds and now this rash..."

"Don't worry about it, Mom-Mom. I can handle it. I'm stronger than you think," I assured her as we pulled up to the employee entrance of the Springfield Mall.

I leaned over and gave her a kiss before getting out of the car. After I shut the door, I leaned in the partially opened window as she called my name.

"Yes?"

She hesitated and then said, "Have a good day."

"I will," I told her, then hurried inside so I wouldn't be late.

"What's up, TJ?" I said to the store manager.

"Hey, Ash," he replied as I helped him push the security gate up.

I flicked the lights on as I headed to the back to put my backpack in my locker. I took my nametag off the top shelf and pinned it on the left side of my white cotton polo shirt with the American Eagle logo. I checked my backpack for my little bag of sunshine before placing it in my locker. I hated that they didn't allow us to put locks on them, but no one had fucked with my shit so far, and if they knew what was good for them, they wouldn't.

"Hi, Danielle," I said, while passing my co-worker as I headed up front to the register.

She didn't even bother to speak; she just gave me a half-ass wave. I don't know why she didn't like me, but I laughed off her attitude like I always did.

"Where do you want me, TJ?"

"The register is fine," he confirmed.

"Cool."

I hated being out on the floor and in the dressing rooms anyway. I spent most days on the register, which allowed me to hook up my friends and occasionally myself when I needed some extra cash. That's probably why Danielle didn't like me; she always got stuck out on the floor restocking whenever she worked with me. She only got on the register when I was off.

*Shit, I was here first. Deal with it!*

The mall opened and it was slow at first, but quickly, things picked up and we were busy. Around noon, my girl Stacey walked through the doors.

"What's up, Ash?" she said when she stopped at the register.

"Hey," I responded.

I never brought attention to my encounters with Stacey. It was best if we appeared to be casual acquaintances instead of roadies. That way, when she brought her shit up to the register, no one paid close attention.

Looking around, I noticed Danielle giving Stacey the evil eye. So, I sent her a quick text message telling her to keep an eye on Miss Newsy Pot. After receiving and reading my text, Stacey moved away from where Danielle was putting clothes on one of the racks.

A customer asked Danielle if she could try some stuff on, and as soon as she went into the dressing room, Stacey made a beeline to the register.

"Thank you, Miss," I said, handing her the bags filled with merchandise we would sort out later when I got to her house.

I rang up one or two items at regular price, but most of the other stuff, I didn't ring at all or I discounted them...deeply. Stacey knew we'd make twice what she paid or more once we sold the shit later on. Of course, the money we made would be used to get more shit from Jake. This was our routine.

"TJ, can you take over the register while I go to the bathroom?"

"Sure, I'll be right out," he replied over the intercom on the phone.

Once he relieved me, I headed back to my locker, grabbed my backpack, and went into one of the bathroom stalls. Using my foot, I knocked the toilet lid down and sat down. I reached inside my backpack, searching for my baggie. It wasn't there! I frantically searched for it, even going as far as dumping my shit out on the floor. As I moved shit around on the floor, a set of feet appeared on the outside of the stall door.

"Looking for this?" a voice said as they waved the bag under the door before snatching back.

*Bam!* I took my foot and kicked the door open, knowing just who had my shit. There she was, now up against the wall from the force of the door hitting her when I kicked it open.

"You bitch!" Danielle screamed.

"Give me my shit," I said through gritted teeth as I lunged towards her.

"You fucking junkie! I should get you fired!"

"What you should do is give me my shit before I fuck you up in here," I warned, as she continued holding my shit hostage in the palm of her hand.

"Here," she said, holding the bag by her fingertips.

When I went to grab it, she did some ole' crazy shit like she was a football player and shot past me, running into the other stall. By now, I was really pissed and started banging on the door she had locked.

"Open this fucking door, Danielle!"

She opened the door just in time for me to see my powder and the plastic pouch it was in floating in the toilet. I lost all sense of reality and went ballistic!

"You fucking, bitch!" I yelled.

I swear I was foaming at the mouth. Grabbing Danielle by her long black hair that was pulled back in a tight ponytail, I slammed her into the wall. The confinement of the tiny space made the impact even harder.

"Get off of me, you crazy bitch!" Danielle screamed, while trying to remove my hand from her hair.

That wasn't even possible, because the grip I had on her needed a fucking crowbar to be released. As my eyes locked on the brown water my powder had become and the baggie that was leisurely circling the porcelain pool, I lost it again.

Still holding her hair, I reached over with my free hand, after punching her in the stomach for trying to break my hold, and lifted the seat so there was nothing in the way as I forced her face into the tainted water. After holding her there almost long enough to drown her, I pulled her up and threw her on the floor outside the stall. Then, I jumped on top of her and commenced to whoop her ass.

Her screams finally brought people back to where we were, and even though the sign clearly read *Employees Only*, the faces staring at me in astonishment were not employees of American Eagle.

Martin, the so-called security guard, finally made his way back there and pulled me off of a very wet and bloody Danielle. He called to TJ on his walkie-talkie and told him to call an ambulance.

"I'm sorry, Ashley," he apologized, while putting a pair of the plastic cuffs he carried for thieves that weren't as smooth as Stacey and I on my wrists. He had to pull them tight because my wrists were small.

The crowd cleared a path as he led me out at the exact same time the paramedics were wheeling a stretcher in for Danielle. I felt no remorse for my actions. That bitch had crossed the line, and she got exactly what she deserved. Danielle went to Springfield Hospital right up the street from the mall, while I got a trip to their police borough.

While being booked, I prayed someone would be there soon to get me. I asked TJ to call my mom or Aunt Chris, screaming their phone numbers out to him as I was being led away. Everywhere I looked all eyes were on me. At that moment, I didn't care. All I wanted was to get to Stacey or even Jake. The men from the *Sopranos* didn't faze me anymore. I needed my shit!

# ❧Chapter Eight❧

"I can't believe you, Ashley!" my mom continued fussing as she drove me home.

"Mom, it's not that serious," I said, trying to calm her down. It didn't work.

"Not that serious! Not that serious! Did I not just pick you up from jail, Ashley?" she yelled.

"They had to take me there, Mom. It's protocol or whatever they call it," I reasoned.

"No, they didn't. If you were at work doing your damn job instead of beating the hell out of your co-worker for I still don't know what, I wouldn't have had to leave my job to come get your ass out of jail," she screamed.

"She started it," I retorted, trying to deter her from asking why I did it.

"So that makes putting her in the hospital okay? What's going on with you, Ashley?" she asked as she began to cry.

"I don't know," I answered barely above a whisper.

She pulled to the side of the road so her blurred vision didn't cause an accident.

"I just don't understand, Ash. How could you go all these years holding in something as serious as Johnny doing that stuff to you?" she asked, turning in the seat to face me.

She couldn't even bring herself to say the words any more than I could.

"I didn't want him to be taken away from Lil' Johnny and Brandon. They needed him..."

"I'm sorry, but they didn't need a sick fuck like that around. Look what he's done to you. All this anger you're holding in has you putting people in the hospital. That's not you, Ash."

I understood where she was coming from, but putting Danielle in the hospital had nothing to do with Johnny's bullshit. Well, maybe in a way it did.

When I didn't respond, she kept talking.

"Why didn't you tell me? Haven't I always protected you? Been there when you needed me? Do you know how this makes me feel? I know it's not about me, but I'm your mother, and I should've been the first to know," she cried hysterically.

"So how come you didn't?" I asked in a tone that sounded as if it came from someone else.

Mom snapped her head up from its position against the steering wheel and stared at me.

"What did you say?"

"I said, how come you didn't know? I came home full of anger after every visit, yet no one seemed to notice. Every time someone came in my room, I was afraid they were there to hurt me...like he did. Yet, no one noticed my fear. That's why I started locking my door all the time," I said as my own tears fell.

I used the back of my hand to wipe the snot running from my nose partially because I was crying, but mostly because of the excessive snorting I was doing. Lately, a runny nose seemed to be my constant companion.

I knew I hit a nerve. I didn't mean to, but the signs were there. No one seemed to notice, though.

Mom pulled out into the afternoon traffic and headed to Mom-Mom's. She put on her sunglasses to block the setting sun and I'm sure to shield her red-rimmed eyes that weren't finished crying.

When I walked through the door, everyone stared at me like I was a monster with two heads.

"What the hell is wrong with you these days?" Pop-Pop yelled.

"Ashley, why would you do such a thing?" Mom-Mom asked.

I was mentally exhausted from the conversation with my mom, but I knew it was no use trying to avoid the questions everyone else had waiting for me.

"They didn't tell you what I was locked up for?"

I was sure they knew the whole story. Now that I thought about it, the charges had been aggravated assault, so maybe they didn't know why I beat Danielle's ass. If I could convince her not to show up at my court case, then I wouldn't have to worry about anyone knowing about the drugs.

"She dumped the stuff in my backpack in the toilet," is all I revealed.

"What? Why would she do such a thing?" Aunt Chris wanted to know.

"She's a hater. She's jealous that TJ always puts me on the register, while she has to work on the floor and in the dressing rooms."

"Well, she won't have to worry about you anymore," Mom chimed in.

"Why not?" I inquired.

"TJ called and said the district manager said you can't come back. They will mail your last check."

"WHAT!" I screamed to the top of my lungs as I kicked over the magazine rack near my foot at the bottom of the steps.

"Pick that shit up, Ashley! What is wrong with you? Are you on drugs?" Pop-Pop yelled.

That was my cue to get myself in check. The last thing I needed was for them to start suspecting I was doing drugs. I picked up the scattered magazines and placed them neatly back in the rack.

"May I be excused?" I asked.

I knew if I just walked away, someone would have something to say about that, too.

"You didn't answer my question, Ashley?"

"Nothing is wrong, Pop-Pop, and no, I'm not on drugs. I'm just stressed," I said and began to cry.

I was stressed—stressed about the shit with my dad, stressed about the mess I had gotten myself in by whooping Danielle's dumb ass, and most importantly, stressed about the fact that I no longer had a job. That last fact meant I wouldn't have any money to pay for my shit. Just thinking about not being able to cop sent me in an emotional tailspin.

"Just go, Ashley," he growled.

I ran upstairs to my room and slammed the door behind me.

"Don't slam another fucking door in this house!" Pop-Pop yelled up the steps.

Boy, I had definitely hit rock bottom with Pop-Pop. He hadn't yelled at me that much in my entire seventeen years.

When I stopped going to Johnny's, Pop-Pop stepped up and became the dad that I needed in my life. He loved that I was his little tomboy. It was a happy medium between not having a grandson at the time and having a granddaughter who loved to play sports. I missed those days when we spent hours in the backyard perfecting my softball game. Everything we used at practice, he bought me for home, too. It didn't matter what the cost. If it helped, and more importantly, made me happy, he purchased it for me.

Tears rolled out of the corners of my eyes and fell on my pale yellow pillowcase. I really let Pop-Pop down when I quit the softball team...Mia, too. I closed my eyes and tried to forget the pain I had caused those who loved me the most. I was slowly feeling the effects of the hit I missed earlier, thanks to Danielle. I was stressed, and thinking about Pop-Pop and Mia wasn't helping. Still, even as I finally drifted off to sleep, my mind wouldn't let go of the past.

Rich, my boyfriend during my sophomore and junior years, made me very happy. For me, that was a big deal because my last boyfriend, Mike, really messed me up. Mia liked Rich, unlike Mike, which was a big plus for me. Because they got along, it allowed me to hang out with my best friend and the love of my life, or so I thought he was. Some school nights, Mia would sleep over and let me use her cell phone to talk to Rich when my phone would cut off. Mom-Mom had Aunt Chris set my phone to shut off at eleven o'clock on school nights. She didn't understand young love. We'd do anything to see each other or talk on the phone.

Mia and I were on the school softball team. In the beginning, Rich supported me. He would come to all my practices and games. Then, out of the blue, he started complaining that softball interfered with our time together. Softball was my favorite sport, which I excelled at. I planned to play in college, so it was important for me to stay focused. I always showed dedication to any sport I played. I loved softball so much that I talked Mia into joining the team.

"I can't, Ash," she kept telling me at first.

She came to the house and played with Pop-Pop and me until I convinced her otherwise.

My days were filled with school, sports, Mia, and Pop-Pop...until Rich. He had a way of convincing me to do whatever he wanted. First, it was with sex, and later, it was with violence.

It was difficult explaining to Pop-Pop why I quit the team a short time later. However, Mia knew because she witnessed firsthand Rich's abusive behavior. He would argue with me before practice, causing me to be off my game.

"Get your head in the game, Ashley!" Coach would yell.

In the locker room, after one really bad practice, Coach pulled me in his office.

"What's going on with you, Ashley? You've been playing too long for you to be making these rookie mistakes. Is everything alright?"

I was about to tell him that I was having a few personal problems, but then I saw Rich standing against the wall when the locker room door swung open. The look on his face let me know I was in for another fight.

"Everything's fine, Coach. I'll do better tomorrow, I promise," I said, then hurried out of his office to a very pissed-off Rich.

"Damn, Ashley! It's not bad enough that I gotta wait around while you have practice, but then, I gotta waste more time while you chit chat with the fucking coach," he yelled as we headed for his car.

"Sorry," I mumbled, sliding in the passenger seat.

"You better be," he said as he reached over and began caressing my thighs.

I wasn't in the mood for sex, but there was no denying Rich. If I didn't want to fight, I made sure to keep him happy.

"I know why the coach wanted you in his office," he whispered in my ear while on top of me in his room.

"What are you talking about?"

"He wants some of this good shit you got," he said, while becoming more aggressive.

"No, he doesn't, Rich. Why would you even say such a thing?" I responded as I tried pushing him off of me. Clearly, he had killed the mood with that comment.

He grabbed my wrist so tightly that I screamed out in pain.

"Are you calling me a liar?" he said, anger apparent in his voice.

"Let go, Rich! You're hurting me," I cried.

Instead, he got rougher. The only thing that stopped him was his sister entering the room without knocking.

"What the fuck are you doing, little brother?" She laughed when she saw him pinning my half-naked body down on the bed.

The distraction caused him to release my wrists and allowed me to get away from him. As he cursed his sister out, who continued laughing at my expense, I grabbed my shit and left.

The next day, he showed up at practice, along with his sister, and goaded me into a big shouting match. Mia pulled me onto the field so I wouldn't get in trouble for being late. It didn't matter anyway. My wrists hurt so badly, I couldn't play worth shit. That sent Coach on a tyrant of his own, and before I realized what I was saying, I quit.

Mia couldn't believe it, and to say Pop-Pop was devastated when I told him that I quit the team doesn't even begin to explain it. I told him that I didn't want to play anymore because I wasn't getting along with the girls on the team, that they were bitchy and catty. I'm sure he knew that was a lie because I had been playing with most of those girls since I started on the PAL league years ago. Truthfully, they were my friends, and they were just as upset about me quitting as everyone else. Everyone except for Rich, that is.

Yes, after all that, I still stayed with him. The more time I spent with Rich, the more he wanted. He began suffocating me. If we were in the school library and one of my friends sat down with us, he got pissed and would tell me to pack up my stuff so we could leave. Like a child, I gathered my things and followed him to avoid a confrontation. He wasn't above lashing out at me in public, but mostly, he did it in private. Dealing with him and his sister, who suddenly hated me, was like a tag team wrestling match.

Like a dummy, I kept going back because Rich kept apologizing and saying how much he loved me and needed me in his life. After Mike's betrayal, I desperately wanted things to work with Rich, so I did whatever he said. That cost me everything and everyone that I loved.

My family got a nasty Ashley instead of the one they knew and loved. My only support person was Aunt Chris, who was always there for me whether she agreed with the situation or not. However, that ended one day when she was in my room while I was dressing and saw the bruises on my back that Rich had caused.

"End it, Ashley! Now!" she told me.

Rich and his sister turned my school days into a living hell. The stress brought my drug use to an all-time high. I started smoking weed and crushing pills daily, and that led to graduating to coke.

Upon waking up, I was immediately filled with feelings of depression.

*I miss Mia so much.*

I leaned over to get my phone and call her. As soon as I raised my finger over the number three, her speed dial number, my phone rang and Stacey's name flashed across the screen. I hit the *Talk* button.

"I thought you were coming by after work," she said, not bothering with a proper greeting.

"I got locked up," I told her matter-of-factly, as if it was no big deal.

Stacey began to panic. "Locked up! For what? Do they know about the clothes?"

"No, I don't think so. I beat the shit out that bitch, Danielle."

"For what? Did she see me?" From her questions, she was clearly worried her ass was in trouble.

"No. That bitch stole my shit out of my bag in my locker and fucking threw in it the toilet," I told her, getting pissed off all over again.

In my agitated state, it didn't take much.

"You're fucking joking, right?"

Again, I answered, "No."

"I know you whooped that ass, right?" Stacey laughed now that she was no longer worried about her own ass.

"You bet I did. I tried to kill that bitch! Did you sell that shit yet?" I asked.

"Most of it. I got a hundred dollars so far," Stacey bragged.

"I'll be right over," I said, then hung up without saying bye.

I grabbed my backpack and tiptoed downstairs, where I heard voices filtering in through the open dining room window. That meant they were outside on the deck. I ran down the last few steps and walked right out the front door.

Around the corner, I sat on the bench at the trolley stop. Thankfully, it came a few minutes later. By the time they realized I wasn't in my room, hopefully, Stacey and I would be on our way back from Jake's. With my fix, I would be able to deal with them a lot easier.

I boarded the trolley with one thing on my mind— getting high.

"Grab the money and meet me on the 102. Run! It'll be at your stop in about six minutes," I commanded when I called Stacey.

She wanted it as badly as I did, so I knew she'd make that trolley, even if she had to step over her own mother to do it.

When we reached her stop, she boarded the trolley breathing heavily. Her wavy hair was loose, and she was dressed in a canary yellow *Juicy Couture* sweat suit. It didn't fit the way it did when I saw her in it the first time; it hung loosely instead of clinging to the curvaceous figure she once had.

She spotted me in the back and made her way in my direction, smiling at me while pulling the flyaway strands from her sweaty face.

"You trying to kill me, girl. You know I'm a smoker. I can't be running like I'm a fucking track star!"

"You are in my book," I told her and gave her a hug. It was enough to stop her complaining.

We rode the rest of the way to Jake's stop in silence while she tried to catch her breath. All earlier thoughts of Mia and how much I missed her had been replaced by one thing—my need to feed.

# ❧Chapter Nine❧

The weatherman didn't lie when he said it was going to feel like summer. It was every bit of eighty degrees on the mid-May afternoon. Yet, I had the chills. Unfortunately, I wasn't outside enjoying the sunny weather because I was stuck in the judge's chambers for the second time in the last month.

My court case with Danielle came up first. I wasn't too worried about it since I had sent word to her that if I ended up with anything other than a slap on the wrist, the beating I gave her would be nothing in comparison to what she would get when I caught up with her. I wasn't allowed back in the store, but the rest of the mall was fair game.

There was no courtroom filled with our respective families. It was just our mothers, a court reporter, our legal representation, and us appearing in front of the judge.

"State your name for the record, please," Judge Michaels ordered.

"Ashley Kennedy," I replied.

"Danielle Martin."

"Stephen Mitchell, Your Honor, representing Ashley Kennedy."

"Lisa Jones, Your Honor, representing Danielle Martin."

"Thank you. You may be seated. Now, I see that Ms. Kennedy has been charged with Aggravated Assault. How do you plead, Ms. Kennedy?"

"Not guilty, Your Honor."

The judge looked up with a puzzled expression. He wasn't expecting that. He had the pictures from Danielle's visit to the ER on his desk, and clearly, someone had beaten her ass.

"Ms. Kennedy, did you or did you not do this to Ms. Martin?" he asked, while showing me the pictures.

"Yes."

"But you're pleading Not Guilty?"

I nodded my head.

"You must speak for the record, Ms. Kennedy," he instructed.

"Yes," I said loudly.

"May I ask how that is possible?"

"Because it was self-defense," I responded, stunning everyone.

I guess Judge Michaels accepted that for the moment, because he moved on to Danielle and her lawyer.

"Ms. Jones," the judge said, indicating it was their turn.

Danielle and her lawyer were whispering, which prompted the judge to clear his throat and call her name again.

"Ms. Jones, are you and your client ready?"

"I'm sorry, Your Honor," Ms. Jones said as she stood up.

"Your Honor, my client has informed me that she wishes to drop the charges against Ms. Kennedy."

Judge Michaels looked stunned by this turn of events. He asked me and Mr. Mitchell to wait outside while he spoke to Danielle and Ms. Jones.

When we got outside, Mr. Mitchell had an "I don't know what the hell just happened" look on his face. I, on the other hand, was perfectly calm. The hit I took before we left home played a big part in it, along with the fact that I knew exactly why Danielle was dropping the charges. One beating was enough for her.

The court reporter came out and asked us to return to the judge's chambers.

"Mr. Mitchell, Ms. Kennedy, please sign the documents in the required places, and you're free to go."

I looked over at Danielle with a smirk on my face. When I walked out to where my mom was waiting, she immediately jumped up.

"How did it go?" she asked.

"Fine," I responded nonchalantly. "She dropped the charges."

"Really?"

Even my mom was surprised because my attorney had showed her the pictures of Danielle from the ER.

"Yeah. I guess she knew she was wrong for starting it," I lied.

She shrugged her shoulders and headed for the exit with me following her.

"Can we go get Timmy and then go to the carnival at the field?"

"I guess so," Mom replied.

We got in the car and headed home to round up Timmy and the rest of the family. There was a carnival a few blocks away at the softball field, and I wanted one day of normalcy. I hadn't spent much quality time with my baby brother lately, and I missed just chilling with him. It turned out to be one of the best days I'd had in a long time. Timmy loved the rides, especially the water slides they had set up. I lost count of how many times we did that one ride.

Now, as I sat in court for the second time, I tried to use those memories with Timmy to keep me calm. I didn't have anything to take before we left for the courthouse. Since losing my job, getting my fix had become a lot harder. I looked around the courtroom at the many faces staring at me. I wanted to run out of there with the quickness, but it was too late for that as the bailiff called court into session.

"All rise for the Honorable Judge Nicholas."

The entire courtroom stood until the judge had been seated.

"Good morning, Counsel, ladies and gentlemen. Today we're here to hear the case of The Commonwealth versus John Wynton on the grounds of Sexual Battery of a Child, Indecent Contact with a Minor, Rape of a Child, Statutory Rape, and Involuntary Deviate Sexual Intercourse with a Child. Does Counsel have any objections to the charges I just read?"

"No, Your Honor," Mr. Mitchell, our family attorney, said.

"No, Your Honor," his attorney, Diane Walters, responded.

"Mr. Mitchell, you may give your opening remarks."

"Thank you, Your Honor. Good morning, ladies and gentlemen. Today I'm here to right a terrible wrong committed against my client, Ashley Kennedy. Ashley is a beautiful seventeen-year-old teenager today, but when this heinous crime was committed..." He paused for effect. "...she was five-years-old."

Gasps could be heard throughout the courtroom.

"Ladies and gentlemen, I caution you to keep all comments and reactions to yourself through the proceedings," Judge Nicholas warned. "Mr. Mitchell, you may continue."

"The defendant, John Wynton, is the father of Ashley Kennedy. We are here today to prove beyond a reasonable doubt that Mr. Wynton crossed a line no parent should ever cross. He sexually abused his trusting five-year-old daughter repeatedly during a four-year period of time while she was in his care for weekend visitations. This is a despicable act, especially from a father to his own daughter, and we will ask the court to seek justice for Ashley Kennedy at the conclusion of this trial. Thank you."

I took a peek over at the jury; they were all staring at me! Under the table, my legs were flapping open and closed as I continued scratching at the always-present rash on my upper arms. I continued biting my lower lip, pulling the dry skin off with my teeth.

*God, I just want this to be over!*

"Good morning, ladies and gentlemen. My name is Diane Walters, and I'm here today to prove that my client, John Wynton, did not do the things Miss Kennedy is accusing him of."

*How could a woman represent this scumbag?*

The look on her face was as if she didn't care what the truth was—my truth. I hated her just as much as I hated my so-called father.

"At no time during the period in question did Mr. Wynton ever do anything other than provide outstanding care for his daughter," she proceeded. "Mr. Wynton has no idea why, after all these years, Miss Kennedy has decided to level these hurtful accusations against him. We hope to get to the bottom of it today. My client would like to return home to his loving family, instead of being locked behind bars as he has been since these accusations were made. Thank you."

She walked back to her place and took a seat next to my father, who hadn't looked my way the entire time we'd been in there.

"Mr. Mitchell, call your first witness," Judge Nicholas ordered.

My lawyer stood to his feet and called on the person who caused all of this—Dr Schultz.

I watched my therapist take a seat on the witness stand next to the judge. She placed her hand on the Bible and swore to tell the truth before taking a seat.

"Dr. Schultz, please tell us how you know the complainant, Miss Kennedy," my lawyer said.

"She's my patient," Dr. Schultz answered. "I'm a Family Therapist. Ashley has been coming to me for about two months now."

"Can you tell the court why you believe you're here, since doctor/patient confidentiality would prohibit you from discussing Miss Kennedy's case?"

"I was subpoenaed by the state to testify," she admitted. "I made a report on behalf of Miss Kennedy."

"Did Miss Kennedy ask you to make this report?" my lawyer asked, while slowly pacing the floor.

"No, sir. It's a requirement based on state law," Dr. Schultz tested. "Whenever a minor makes an accusation of sexual abuse, we are obligated to report it to the Children and Youth Protective Services."

"And you did this after your first encounter with Miss Kennedy?"

"No. I actually waited until her third session before I made the report," she admitted.

"And why was that?" My lawyer stopped his pacing directly in front of her. He folded his arms across his chest and waited for her to answer.

"Well," Dr. Schultz started to explain as she repositioned herself in her seat, "Miss Kennedy did not reveal the true reason for her visit until moments before our first session ended. I felt at the time I didn't have enough information to go on to make such a report, so I waited."

"I see," my lawyer said. "Why not make the report after her second session?"

"During the second session, she was reluctant to provide any real details until close to the end of our allotted time...just as she did the first time. I decided to ask her to bring her mother with her to the next session, hoping to get a clearer understanding of what was going on."

"So, during your first two sessions her mother was not in attendance?"

"No, her aunt Christine accompanied her," Dr. Schultz replied. "Christine was the one who contacted me to set up the sessions. She said her niece felt more comfortable coming with her. As long as the patient is accompanied by an adult, there isn't usually a problem."

The questioning continued, and everything Dr. Schultz said was accurate. After my lawyer finished up, my dad's lawyer stood to her feet for her cross-examination.

"Dr. Schultz," she started, "you told us all about your encounters with Miss Kennedy and her family.

Did you not make the report immediately after the admittance because you didn't believe Miss Kennedy was in any imminent danger?"

"No. I didn't make the report based solely on the fact that I didn't have any concrete evidence except a distraught teenager saying seconds before running out of my office that she was molested by her father," Dr. Schultz replied confidently.

"So the accusation itself wasn't enough?" Ms. Walters prodded.

"I guess it should've been, but I like to have more than just one sentence to go on."

"That's a pretty damaging sentence, don't you think, Dr. Schultz?" Ms. Walters said as she walked back over to the table where Johnny sat with a smug look on his face.

*Bullshit!* I wanted to shout out. *That bitch is trying to fuck up what was said.*

My lawyer had warned me about this, but to actually see it happening burned me up inside.

The sounds of movement and whispers among those seated in the courtroom became a tad bit noticeable after that remark.

"Order in the court," the judge ordered. "Are you

finished, Ms. Walters?"

"Yes, Your Honor," she confirmed.

"Let's take a ten-minute recess," Judge Nicholas decided after staring at my distraught face.

I jumped up and made a beeline for the nearest exit. My mom and Mr. Mitchell were right on my heels.

"Ashley! Ashley!" Mom called out to me.

I swear I had one foot out the door. My nerves were so on edge that I felt like I was about to explode, and my fucking rash wasn't making things any easier. It felt like my skin was on fire. I needed a hit so bad that I would have done just about anything if someone offered me one at that moment.

My mom caught up to me and turned my unwilling body around in the direction of the room where Mr. Mitchell was waiting for us.

"Ashley, I know this is tough on you, but just hang in there a little longer," he coached. "Once you tell your side of the story, the jury and every person in that courtroom will see things clearly. All you have to do is tell the truth when it's your turn."

"I don't think I can do this," I cried.

My mom took me in her arms and held me tightly. For a moment, I felt safe again. Her arms shielded me from the world.

*Why did I ever open my mouth?* It was a question I asked myself a lot before this nightmare ended. *This is only going to get worse.*

The recess ended. We took our seats back at the table and waited for Judge Nicholas to reappear.

We stood, we sat, and for another hour, the lawyers went back and forth with their questioning. Next on the hot seat had been Mr. Tyler and Ms. Chancellor from Child Services. They told the court what happened when they paid us a visit. Ms. Chancellor spoke about the fact that Mom-Mom and Pop-Pop had no idea about the accusations I had made. His lawyer had a field day with that. She couldn't understand why they would've been kept in the dark when both Aunt Chris and my mom knew before they showed up to the house.

"Why all the secrecy?" she asked.

Again, mumbles could be heard throughout the semi-packed courtroom.

*Did total strangers really show up just to watch other people's misery?* I thought to myself.

After that testimony, we broke for lunch. I didn't bother to eat anything. Food wasn't what I craved. As nervous as I was, I would have probably ended up throwing it up anyway.

While everyone else ate the ordered-in lunch, Mr. Mitchell sat with me to go over my testimony. I tried concentrating on what he was saying, but he had something stuck in his too big front teeth that kept distracting me. The toupee he wore didn't help either. I tried to focus on something behind him, but he kept turning around to see what I was staring at.

After lunch, we returned to the courtroom. Next on the stand was Aunt Chris. She told her version of how it happened, and again, that bitch of a lawyer tried to switch the story around.

Ms. Walters began her interrogation from her seat, and she made it short and sweet.

"Mrs. Clarkson, are you always in the habit of acting as Miss Kennedy's confidante?"

"I guess you could say that. We're very close," Aunt Chris answered.

"So, if that's true, can you tell me why she confided in you the night she saw her father recently, but had not said one word about this alleged abuse to you in all the years since she claimed this happened?"

The look on Aunt Chris' face clearly told me that she wanted to jump out that seat and whoop Ms. Walters' ass the same way I had beat Danielle's. Instead, she kept her composure and politely answered the question.

"I don't know, Ms. Walters. You'll have to ask her."

"That will be all."

"Mr. Mitchell, would you like to redirect?" the judge asked.

"No, Your Honor."

"Mrs. Clarkson, thank you. You may step down."

Judge Nicholas looked at the clock, and thankfully, he decided he had enough for one day. I know I damn sure did. From the looks on the faces of the rest of my family, I assumed they felt the same way. I don't care what positive bullshit Mr. Mitchell was spouting off to us...shit was not looking good.

We sat there and let the courtroom clear out before making our way outside. There were no reporters waiting to shove microphones in our faces or photographers waiting to snap our pictures. I was a *nobody* and this story wasn't headline news. The only people who cared what happened in this case were my family...and his.

# ❧Chapter Ten❧

As soon as we got home from the courthouse, I took a shower and changed into something more comfortable. I wasn't sure if it was the temperature or just the feeling of disgust I felt after spending hours in the same space as my so-called father, but my skin was crawling. I had scratched so much my arms looked like someone threw boiling water on me. The skin on my upper arms and thighs were bright red and blistered. While looking in the partially steam-covered bathroom mirror, I saw were it was beginning to spread to my back. I grabbed the hydrocortisone cream and slathered it all over my infected skin. I needed some on my back, but I didn't want Mom-Mom to see how bad it had gotten. So, I decided to take the cream with me when I left and have Stacey put it on for me.

Thankfully, the doctor didn't run any test on my blood or urine, opting to just assume it was an allergic reaction to our detergent or maybe the dye in my clothes. He even mentioned the possibility of bed bugs after I slyly brought it up. As long as he didn't order a drug test, I was safe.

I looked over at my new mattress and box spring they bought me after the doctor mentioned the bed bug scenario. They inspected my old one, and of course, didn't find anything other than lots of my dead skin cells. I guess they didn't want to take any chances, though. I felt guilty for letting Mom-Mom and Pop-Pop spend that kind of money on a lie, but I wasn't about to tell them the truth.

With each passing day, I was becoming someone even I didn't recognize. When the sun rose in the morning, it was anyone's guess which Ashley I would be. My family had gotten use to the mood swings I exhibited at any given moment; so much so that they just ignored me when I started acting crazy.

The only person I controlled myself around was my baby brother. I don't know what it was, but whenever I looked at him, my protective instincts kicked in. I wasn't about to let anyone hurt him, not even me. It didn't matter how fucked up I felt on the inside; when he was around, I was Miss Mary Sunshine on the outside. If I forgot for one minute and snapped out on him, I spent the rest of the day making it up to him. In his eyes, I was his big sister and he loved me. I never wanted that to change and I made sure it didn't.

Timmy was kept away from the latest family drama by his dad, Jimmy. He was a godsend to my mom...and me, too. I know he hated everything I was putting my mom through lately. Yet, he never treated me any differently. The fact that I already had one asshole of a dad was probably what kept him from going off on me whenever I upset my mom.

Enough of the pity party. I needed something, and standing around there wasn't going to help me get it. I pulled my hair up in a loose bun, threw on my blue and white maxi dress, and slipped into a pair of gold flats. I put on a white lightweight sweater that had quarter-length sleeves to cover up the rash. The last thing I needed was people staring at me with their noses turned up. I didn't need to catch another case. It seemed lately, I was having a hard time controlling my temper, and when I hadn't had a fix in over twenty-four hours, it was damn near impossible.

"Mom-Mom, can I borrow your car for a little while?" I asked when I got downstairs where she and Pop-Pop were sitting at the kitchen table.

She sighed deeply, but tossed me the keys anyway. Pop-Pop just looked at me and shook his head. He didn't have much to say one way or the other these days. I had no idea how I was going to repair the damage I had done to our relationship. I pushed those thoughts to the side momentarily and concentrated on the task at hand—finding a fix.

"Hey, girl, what's up?" I asked when Stacey answered her cell.

"Nothing much."

"You got anything?" I didn't have to be specific; she knew what I meant.

"Nope, I'm busted, and Jake ain't trying to take no I.O.U.s," she replied.

"I got to get something or I'm going to be sick."

"Wish I could help you, Ash, but all I have is some weed and a few Percs. If you don't find anything, hit me back and I'll split this with you. A high is a high when you're sick."

"Yeah, you're right. Let me see what I can find. I'll hit you back later."

"Alright," she said and we hung up.

I was about to call Jake, but decided a pop-up visit may get me better results. I bypassed Stacey's block and kept heading in the direction of Lansdowne Avenue. I parked in our usual spot around the corner, taking a moment to apply some gloss to my dry lips before getting out the car. As I neared the side entrance, I noticed the door was slightly ajar. Angry voices could be heard from inside.

"Muthafucka, how dare you try to cheat us!"

I stopped in my tracks when I heard a male voice sternly say, "We've been good to you! Bringing you our primo shit and selling it to you for a fair cut of the profit, and this is what you do!"

"Yo, Max, ain't nobody tryin' to cheat y'all. I'm paying you what you charged me. What difference does it make what I make on the back end?" Jake's voice I recognized.

"I should pop a cap in your ass right now," another voice spoke up.

"Yo, Wayne, chill with that shit! If it's more money you want, I'll get it." I heard Jake doing something I never expected...bitchin' up.

"You got one week to get us double our original price or when we come back...there will be no conversation."

My heart began to beat frantically as the gentlemen neared the open door. Quickly, I ran back to the hedges surrounding the front of Jake's parents' house and did my best to hide. I didn't know where their car was because it wasn't in the driveway. After they walked past where I was crouched down, I overheard one of them say to the other, "When we come back, with or without our cash, this greedy muthafucka is dead."

I was already feeling sick from not having my fix, but hearing them plotting to kill Jake had my stomach in knots. I felt the bile rising to my throat. I put my hand over my mouth to muffle the sound when I saw the men look back in my direction before getting in a black Cadillac parked at the curb. As soon as they pulled off, my insides—what little was in there—emptied into my hand.

I didn't know what to do. *Should I get the hell out of here before anyone knows I overheard what just happened? Or should I be loyal to Jake and tell him the men are plotting his demise?*

I was there for a fix, and one way or another I planned to get it. Right then, I had a trump card to play. Never without something for my runny nose, I reached in my bag and fished out a crumpled-up tissue. I wiped my vomit-smelling hand off as best I could and left my hiding spot. After knocking on the security screen door, I waited for Jake to answer. The usually locked steel door was still slightly ajar, only a little more than a few minutes ago since the plus-sized men had just exited it.

"What the fuck you want?" Jake asked when he saw me at his door.

"I need some shit...bad," I told him.

"What happened to calling first? You know the rules," he said, then began closing the door in my face.

"I overheard those men talking about you."

He froze. Standing there, he looked at me for a few minutes before responding to my comment.

"And?"

"And I'm sure you'd be interested in what they were saying," I responded with cockiness.

He didn't say anything; he just unlocked the door and moved to the side to allow me to enter. Drugs were all over the bar. My eyes lit up like a kid in a candy store.

"How much you need?" he asked, thinking I was there to buy some.

*Never ask an addict how much they need. No matter how much we consume...it's never enough.*

"I don't have any money," I answered truthfully.

"So what the fuck are you doing here?" he yelled, clearly pissed off.

"I thought I could strike a bargain."

He laughed. "With what? What the fuck could you have that I would want?"

"This," I said, pointing to my body, "but then as luck would have it, my hand just got a lot better thanks to Max and Wayne."

"Oh really? I see you remembered their names. Pretty good for only hearing them one time."

"Truth be told, I heard them twice," I confessed. "When you were arguing with them just now."

"Eavesdropping, huh?" he said with his brows furrowed.

"Not intentionally," I replied.

"So what's this card you have to play?"

"How about you give me a little taste to help with this sickness, and then we can bargain for a little more?" I asked hopefully.

"How about you go in the bathroom and do something about that vomit smell that you brought in here with you?" Jake said nastily. "It's turning my stomach."

I sucked my teeth and headed to the back where his bathroom was located. I closed the door behind me and sat down on the closed toilet lid. Just like the rest of the place, his bathroom was masculine and very upscale. Everything was black and gold. The sink was one of those new ones that looked like a bowl on top of a dresser, and the toilet was oval shaped and low to the floor with an automatic flushing sensor. The tile floor was a black marble pattern, and the two throw rugs were gold and matched the design in the shower curtain.

Careful not to make a mess, I washed my hands and face with one of the extra cloths I found on the gold towel bar beside the sink. I put some of his toothpaste on my fingertip and swooshed it around my mouth. Placing my hands under the running faucet, I managed to get enough water in them to slurp up and rinse my mouth out before going back to join Jake at the bar.

In my absence, he had begun cleaning up all the drugs that were sprawled out everywhere moments ago. A ten-dollar hit of heroin lay on the end of the bar nearest the empty seat I occupied a few minutes ago.

"For me?" I asked coyly.

"Yeah," he grumbled. "Now start talking."

"Oh no, not yet. First, I need to know what I'm getting in exchange for this information," I joked.

"You get to leave with all your body parts still attached," he stated threateningly.

"Don't be like that, Jake," I said, moving closer to him seductively.

"Really, little girl?" he replied, trying to demean me.

"Little girl my ass," I snapped back. "Stop acting like you haven't been checking me out since the first day we met."

"Whatever," he said with a hint of a smirk on his face.

That was my cue to try a little harder. Since I didn't have a job, I was broke. So, whatever I could con out of Jake needed to be enough to at least get me through the next couple of days. The case against my father would pick back up in two days. I definitely needed something to get me through that shit.

I walked up to Jake and stood behind him. He had me by a couple inches, but our waists were in close enough proximity that I was able to lean into him and wrap my arms around his waist.

"What are you doing?" he inquired, turning slightly to look at me. The tone of his voice had softened considerably.

"Something you're obviously too scared to do," I teased.

"You think so?" he asked.

He turned to face me, and in one swift movement, he lifted me in the air and placed me on top of the bar. The next thing I knew, my sandals were making a loud clang as they each hit the floor. My maxi dress became a necklace around my neck as Jake pushed it there to give himself better access to all I was offering. Of course, that was after he promised to give me what I needed. To prove he wasn't lying, he gave me some while we were doing it, which heightened the pleasure to a level I'd never experienced. He also stopped his attack on my young teenage body long enough to drop a few packets in my backpack in good faith.

Once I knew I had what I came for, I gave him what he wanted. It was a small price to pay, believe me. The sickness that was creeping up on me from not having what my body craved would have been hard to hide. It was only by the grace of God that my family hadn't found out I was on drugs. Saying God had something to do with it probably wasn't right, but I do know it was him that made sure I hadn't OD'd yet.

I spent the few hours with Jake having sex and getting high off his supply. The sex had him twisted to the point that I don't think he realized how much we were doing and how much he gave me to take home. By the time I left, I was high as a fucking kite.

I finally got around to telling him what I overhead Max and Wayne say about killing him. He said he appreciated it, and I guess he showed me just how much.

I don't know how I made it home. Stop signs looked like red lights. I sat at the stop signs until someone behind me began laying on their horn. Mailboxes on the corner looked like people, but somehow I made it home.

Sadly, as I pulled up in front of the house, that's when my luck ran out. I passed out behind the wheel shortly after placing the gearshift in park. The car was still running when someone came outside and found me unconscious behind the steering wheel. I guess God's grace on me had finally run out, too.

# ❦Chapter Eleven❦

I had no idea where I was, but the dull flicker of the fluorescent bulbs over my head should've been a telltale sign. I rolled a little to the left and came face to face with a silver aluminum pole. The blue box with the digital numbers increasing in small increments gave away my vital signs.

While trying to move my right arm, I immediately felt a shooting pain. I turned to see what was causing it. The needle, which disappeared into my vein, was covered with see-through medical tape and attached to clear tubing that led to the double bags of fluids hanging from another aluminum pole positioned silently above my head.

"Hello, Miss Kennedy," a nurse in pink scrubs said as she began checking the numbers on the display.

She pulled the black Velcro blood pressure cuff from the wall and wrapped it around the arm that didn't have the IV attached to it. I watched as she continually squeezed the bulb while listening through her stethoscope.

"One twenty over eighty. Much better than when you got here," she told me, while placing the cuff back in its holder.

Next, she put a disposable cover over the thermometer that hung from a spiral cord on the portable machine she pulled from her pocket. While she had her fingers on my wrist, I finally realized no one from my family was around.

"Where's my family?" I asked.

She held up one finger on her free hand.

"Sorry. If I stopped to answer you, I would've had to start all over again. The doctor just sent them to the cafeteria for some coffee. They've been here all night waiting for you to wake up. They should be back shortly," she answered, as if she just knew they would return.

I, on the other hand, wasn't quite sure. I didn't even remember how I ended up there, but I'm sure it wasn't good.

"What happened?" I asked the nurse.

"You overdosed," she told me as calmly as if she was letting me know it was sunny outside.

"What?" I shouted.

"Yeah. According to your chart, they found you passed out behind the wheel."

I didn't know if it was the sickening aroma that seemed to be the norm in a hospital or the fact that my family now knew my secret that made me begin to heave. The nurse quickly grabbed the gold basin from the over-the-bed table that was pushed to the side and jammed it under my chin. Her timing was perfect; the yellow bile mixed with clear fluid poured from my mouth.

At just that moment, it seemed like a dark cloud moved in front of the sun. I looked up with remnants of vomit dripping from my bottom lip and saw four pair of eyes staring at me from the doorway. My stomach betrayed me once more as another bout of nausea hit me. I just closed my eyes; I couldn't look at them anymore.

A few minutes later, I felt a warm rag on my face. I opened my eyes and was surprised to see Aunt Chris dipping the rag in a clean basin filled with warm water. Next to it was a small bottle of Johnson's Baby Bath.

*Boy, what I wouldn't give to be a baby right now.*

I dared to look over at the three remaining members of this family unit. All of their faces looked so worn and tired. I couldn't imagine what they were thinking. My mom approached the bed first, and I braced myself for whatever she was going to say. She stood there just staring into my face for what felt like forever. The room was so silent, I swear I heard the ticking of the hands on the black and white clock that hung on the slate grey wall in front of me. The silence was shattered by the cries that suddenly left her mouth, startling us all.

"Ashley," she whispered as her tears fell.

Aunt Chris grabbed Mom and embraced her, trying her best to comfort her. As her cries escalated, she pulled away and walked aimlessly around the room.

"What did I do wrong?" she cried out.

"It's not your fault, Marie. She made this choice," Pop-Pop's powerful voice echoed in the hollow room.

When he looked at me with his own red-rimmed eyes, I knew he was not just angry. He was devastated. He walked over to the side of my bed and stared right into my eyes.

"How could you, Ashley? How could you do this to yourself? To us? Haven't we given you everything?"

As he pleaded for an explanation, I just stared at him. I didn't have an answer that he would understand. He didn't know my pain, my struggle. No one did.

"You finished school six months early, so I know you're smart," he continued when I didn't respond to the first set of questions. "So how could you be so dumb?"

He slammed his fist on the table, causing the now cold water in the basin to slosh around inside. He walked out of the room, and finally, Mom-Mom stepped forward and took his place.

"Please don't," I cried as I looked up into her face.

"Heroin, Ashley? Don't you know you're breaking our hearts?"

"Yes, Mom-Mom, I know, and I'm so sorry. If I could stop, don't you think I would?" I cried out angrily.

"How long have you been doing this, Ashley?" she asked.

I hesitated while making the decision as to whether I would tell her the truth or lie. After a few minutes, I decided it was in my best interest to lie. I didn't think they would be able to handle the truth. If they believed it was a one-time thing, maybe we could move on. It was just one big mistake, bad judgment on my part. If I told them how long I had been getting high on heroin alone, things would've never been the same, and we're not even talking about all the other shit I'd done.

"It was the first time, Mom-Mom."

"Well, I guess you must've really enjoyed it," she commented sarcastically.

"Why you say that?" I asked.

"The doctor said if we didn't find you when we did, you would be dead. On top of that, we found more bags of it in your backpack."

*Shit! Please tell me that you didn't do something stupid like get rid of it!*

"It's gone," she said, answering my unasked question.

I felt sick all over again. The dry heaves started immediately. Aunt Chris held my hair back and rubbed circular patterns around the middle of my back as I vomited into the basin. My mom stared out of the window, but the slight movement of her shoulders let me know that she was crying again. This time, she decided to do it privately.

Mom-Mom walked out of the room. Maybe she went in search of Pop-Pop or just needed to get away from her lying, drug-taking granddaughter. I didn't know which.

I was kept under observation for twenty-four hours before being released. The attending physician gave my mom a list of drug rehab centers in the area. He advised her to look into them immediately.

"The amount of drugs in her urine indicates this is not a one-time use situation. She's lucky someone came along when they did, and more importantly, that she didn't kill someone," he told her, while handing her the discharge papers.

The ride home was as dreadful as I knew it would be. Mom had to pull over at least three times during the normally twelve-minute ride from the hospital to Mom-Mom's.

"Ashley, please help me understand what is going on with you," she cried as we pulled up to the house.

"How can you understand something you can't feel?" I asked angrily as I pulled the door handle preparing to jump out.

"Close the fucking door, Ashley!"

Her outburst took me by surprise. I closed the door and sat back prepared for more questions.

"I don't know what the hell is going on with you, but as soon as this trial is over, you're going to rehab! I had enough, and I *know* Mom-Mom and Pop-Pop certainly have had enough of this shit!" Her breathing got heavier as she continued her rampage. "Have you thought about what this will do to this family if something happens to you? What about your baby brother? Do you want him to grow up without his big sister looking at for him? Huh, Ashley?"

I sit silently in the seat next to her. She swelled up with anger, looking as if she was ready to beat me like she did when I was little and got in trouble. A second later, she blew out all the air she held in her lungs. It was like I could actually see her insides deflate.

She snatched the keys out of the ignition and got out the car, slamming the door behind her. I sat there not sure what the hell to do. From the cars parked outside, I knew everyone was home. Finally, I got out and went inside, prepared to take my lumps. Instead, I was greeted by the smile of my baby brother. When he ran and jumped in my arms, I hugged him as tightly as his little arms were wrapped around my neck.

"Ash-yee, where you been? I wanna go to playground," he told me.

"Let's go," I replied.

I didn't bother saying anything to anyone else. We just turned around and walked out the door.

We walked up the street to the neighborhood playground where Timmy and I spent some much-needed quality time together. With the threat of rehab in my immediate future, I didn't know when we would have this time again.

# ❧Chapter Twelve❧

Waking up Monday morning to overcast skies did nothing for my mood. By the time we were ready to walk out the house, it was pouring down raining. As I looked out the window on the ride to the courthouse, I couldn't imagine my life getting any worse...but it did.

Having been in the courtroom for an hour or so, both lawyers had already questioned my mom. Mr. Mitchell asked basic questions about how she met my dad, why they broke up, when did I begin visiting him on my own, and when did the visits stop. He also asked about any noticeable changes in my behavior during that time, along with how she felt when she found out about the accusations.

She had been crying over me so much lately that it didn't take much to get the waterworks started. She seemed to have gone through an entire box of tissues by the time she left the stand. Especially after Ms. Walters started in on her.

"Mrs. Miller, you stated that Mr. Wynton was overly possessive and abusive, causing you to end your relationship with him. Is that correct?"

"Yes, it is," Mom answered.

"So please tell the court why you would feel comfortable leaving your young child in his care?"

"He was her father. I didn't expect him to harm *her*!"

"Why did it take so long for her weekend visits to begin? The two of you had broken up six months earlier, right?" Ms. Walters probed.

"Yes. We broke up about six months before her first overnight stay. It took so long because he never showed up to get her when he said he would. After a few times of being a no-show, she didn't want to go and I didn't force her," Mom stated.

"So why did you eventually let her go then?"

"Because he kept calling me begging to see her. I figured if he was calling that much, he might actually show up. I didn't tell her in case he didn't show. He showed, and she was happy to see him. So, I let her go."

"So you had no reservations at that time about her going with him for the weekend?"

"No, I didn't," Mom answered.

"So when did things change? Why did Miss Kennedy stop visiting her father?"

"She came home after a weekend visit, and for the entire week, she got in trouble at school for fighting. She even wet her bed a couple times."

"Was this normal behavior for her?" Ms. Walters wanted to know.

"Absolutely not! When I asked her what was wrong, she wouldn't tell me. When I began packing her bag for her visit with her father, she kept pulling the clothes back out the bag. I asked her why she was doing that, and she told me she didn't want to go there anymore."

"Did you ask her why?"

Mom looked at her like, *What do you think*, before she answered.

"Yes. I asked her and she began crying. Then she told me that some bad men kept beating up her daddy."

"So let me get this straight. She told you someone was hurting her daddy, but not that her daddy was hurting her?"

Mom's head fell forward as she understood the implication Ms. Walters just made.

She repeated the question, and this time, Mom simply replied, "Yes."

"Thank you, Ms. Miller. That will be all," she stated smugly, then walked back to the table while smirking at my dad.

"Let's take a ten-minute recess," Judge Nicholas said.

We stood until he entered his chambers. Then Mr. Mitchell ushered us into the room we occupied last week.

"Don't worry! Don't worry!" he began excitedly. "Ashley will take care of everything once she takes the stand," he assured us.

"I'm not doing it," I said barely above a whisper.

All heads turned in my direction.

"Excuse me?" Mr. Mitchell asked.

"I said I'm not doing it," I repeated a little louder this time.

"Ashley, sweetheart, you must testify or the jury will not believe your claims," my attorney said.

"They won't believe me anyway. That woman has them eating out the palm of her hands."

"That's why you must testify," my mom interjected, placing her arm around my shoulder. "If you want him to pay for what he did, you have to, Ash."

I looked into her eyes. She was pleading with me. She didn't want him to get away with it for one more minute—and neither did I.

"Okay," I finally said.

We quickly headed back to our respective seats after recess. My nerves had taken over my body. My stomach felt as if it had fallen out of me and onto the floor. I was frozen in fear. Where were my drugs! My rash picked that moment to remind me of its presence. I guess it was a reaction from all the adrenaline flowing through my veins. I sat there staring at Mr. Mitchell and scratching my arms until he repeated himself.

"The prosecution calls Ashley Kennedy to the stand."

Slowly, I rose from my seat at the table and took that long walk to the seat opposite the judge. The bailiff reached out and assisted me as I actually stumbled up the two steps leading to what I felt was the execution box.

"Please state your name for the record," Mr. Mitchell instructed.

"Ashley Kennedy," I whispered.

"Please speak into the microphone," Judge Nicholas leaned over and whispered to me.

"Ashley Kennedy," I repeated, leaning in to the microphone this time.

"How old are you, Miss Kennedy?"

"Seventeen," I answered.

"So you know why we're here today and you understand the consequences of being untruthful then?" The judge looked me directly in the eye.

Nodding, I responded, "Yes."

I could feel my chest heaving as I took each deep breath.

"Would you please tell the court why you are here today?"

I looked over at Johnny and back at Mr. Mitchell, who nodded his salt-and-pepper covered head ever so slightly while adjusting his navy blue suit jacket.

"Because I was molested."

"And do you see the person who molested you here in the courtroom today?"

"Yes," I said, this time making sure to speak into the microphone.

"Can you point this person out?"

I lifted my trembling left hand and pointed my finger at Johnny. As soon as he locked eyes with me, I turned away from his frightening stare.

"Let the record show that the witness has pointed to the defendant John Wynton," my lawyer announced to the courtroom.

People shifting in their seats could be heard in the gallery.

"Ashley, please tell the court why you have made these allegations against Mr. Wynton...your father," he continued.

"Because he hurt me and I couldn't hide it anymore," I said, my voice cracking.

"How long had you been hiding this?" Mr. Mitchell asked.

"Twelve years."

Again, gasps and mumbles erupted.

"Order," Judge Nicholas said, banging his gavel.

"Why did you keep this a secret for so long?" my lawyer continued.

"I didn't think anyone would believe me," I answered as I began scratching again.

"Can you tell us what he did?"

I didn't answer right away; I just bit down on my bottom lip hard enough to make it bleed.

"Ashley?" he prodded.

I looked around at the strangers staring at me and refused to speak. Mr. Mitchell approached me and asked if I'd like the others to leave. I shook my head that I would.

"Your Honor, may I have a sidebar please?"

Judge Nicholas nodded, indicating for Ms. Walters to step forward, and the three of them conversed quietly.

"I think under the circumstances that it would be best if we cleared the courtroom except for immediate family," Mr. Mitchell requested.

The judge looked at Ms. Walters, who nodded her consent.

"Bailiff, please clear the courtroom quickly while Miss Kennedy gives her testimony."

I used those few minutes to recollect my thoughts. *You can do this. He can't hurt you anymore.*

Once the others were gone, we continued.

"He would come in my room when I was asleep and crawl in bed beside me," I explained. "I would wake up because his touching was hurting me. I would feel his hands on my private area."

I answered as if I only had the vocabulary of a five-year-old.

"Did he only touch you with his hands?"

The more he questioned me, the more uncomfortable I got. But, I knew I had to finish what I started.

"No," I admitted as a few tears fell. "He rubbed his private parts against me," I revealed after a long pause.

"Did you tell him to stop? That he was hurting you?"

"Yes," I whispered.

"Did he stop once you told him?"

"No," I responded with another one-word answer.

I wasn't making it easy for Mr. Mitchell. It wasn't easy for me either.

"Did he do anything else besides touch you down there?"

"Yes. He put his hand over my mouth so I couldn't scream. He touched my breast area, too, although there was nothing there," I answered, feeling like I wanted to vomit as the memories flooded my mind.

*God I need a hit! That's the only thing that will make my jitters go away.*

"Did anyone else see what he was doing?" he asked as he walked to the table and picked up a folder.

"Not at first," I recalled. "He would put his finger up to his lips and tell me to be quiet if he heard someone close by. But..."

"But what, Ashley?" My lawyer walked back towards me and leaned against the panel.

"But, after a while, he started..." Tears trickled down my face as the memories came back to me clear as day. "He started letting other people touch me."

The courtroom erupted with sounds of disbelief. I saw my grandmother and Johnny's wife, Angie, staring at me with their mouths gaped open. Thankfully, they had the sense not to bring my little brothers. I'm sure Lil' Johnny may have some recollection of his father's disgusting behavior, but I would never subject him to any of this. If it meant the difference between Lil' Johnny being scarred for life or Johnny going free...I'd let him go free before hurting my little brother. They were the ones I protected all these years by not telling anyone.

"Can you elaborate a little about your last statement for us?" my lawyer asked as he walked over by the jury pit.

After a very long pause, I told the worst of it.

"Him and his friends would be so high that they would take turns passing me down what they called their *Soul Train* line. Each one pretended to dance with me, but really it was just an excuse to touch me...everywhere. They touched me the same way he did when we were alone. If I refused, he beat me. And..." I hesitated to continue.

"Go ahead," Mr. Mitchell encouraged.

"He let the woman kiss on me in front of him. He rubbed on himself while he watched," I finished, the tears and snot blending together while travelling down my lips.

I guess Mr. Mitchell felt that was enough. He stopped there and I hoped that was it.

For a split second, I forgot all about Ms. Walters until Judge Nicholas said, "Ms. Walters, your witness."

She cleared her throat, stood up, adjusted her black pencil skirt, and straightened her silk pink blouse before approaching me.

"Hi, Ashley," she said, trying to sound sweet and caring.

I didn't respond.

"I just have a couple questions. Then this will be over. Okay?" she said, trying to lull me into a false sense of security.

"Okay."

"Now, you said your dad climbed into bed with you, right?"

"Yes."

"Can you tell us a little about the room at your dad's?"

"It was painted pink and white with princess characters on the wall. A pink rug, white dresser, and a lamp with a princess shade."

"So he had a nice room for you there?" she asked.

"Yes."

"What size was the bed? Big or small?"

"It was a twin," I answered, a little confused by the line of questioning.

"So, in that small bed, your big daddy would have to get close to lie down with you, right?"

"I guess so," I responded.

"So, isn't it possible he got a little too close because the bed was so small?"

"No," I answered vehemently.

"Okay, let me ask you something else then. If your dad was doing all this stuff to you— touching you, hurting you, letting his friends touch you—why did you keep going back?"

I didn't hesitate to answer. "Because whenever I made him mad, he took it out on my little brothers to get back at me. I didn't want them to suffer because of me."

"And when you told your mom that you didn't want to go back anymore, did you worry about them getting hurt then?"

"I don't remember," I defensively said.

"You don't remember?" she accused. "Okay. Well, your mom testified that you told her some men hurt your dad and you didn't want to go back," she said, walking over to the table to check her notes. "Why didn't you tell her about what your dad was doing to you? It was the perfect opportunity, especially since she didn't force you to go back after that."

"I told you why," I said as a new batch of tears fell.

I looked at my family. My mom, Mom-Mom, and Aunt Chris were all wiping their eyes. Pop-Pop had opted to stay out in the hall; he didn't want to hear my testimony.

"I have one final question, Ashley."

I looked at her in anticipation. Like an expert swordsman, she delivered the fatal blow.

"Your little brothers are only two and three years younger than you, respectively. So why did you wait twelve years before you told someone? They surely would've been able to alert someone to their father's abusive behavior towards them long before now, don't you think? Their collaboration would've made your story a lot more credible," she said, then glided back to the table and took her seat next to a smug-faced Johnny.

"That'll be all." Her voice seemed to sing the words.

"Mr. Mitchell, anything further?" the judge inquired.

"No, Your Honor. The prosecution rests," he said as he patted me on the back upon my return to the table.

The rest of the trial went by in a blur. My grandmother was placed on the stand, where she told everyone what a wonderful and loving father Johnny had always been. How he was heartbroken and devastated when I stopped visiting. She made him sound like a choirboy. What a fucking joke!

When he got on the stand, I became deaf. I couldn't listen to one word of his lies.

Finally, the testimonies were finished, closing arguments had been made, and the jury had been given their instructions.

The charges leveled against Johnny were first-degree felonies and carried sentences ranging from a term of imprisonment decided by the court of no more than forty years and up to a maximum of life imprisonment.

I knew it was wishful thinking to hope he never saw the outside of a prison cell for the rest of his sorry-ass life. What I didn't expect was the jury to take what was equivalent to a lunch break before coming back with a verdict.

We all filed back into the courtroom, and for the last time, did our sit, stand, sit routine for the judge. The jury took their respective seats, and the foreman, an older gentleman that looked like he had one too many lunches, handed the bailiff a tiny slip of paper that held Johnny's fate.

"Mr. Foreman, please read the verdict," Judge Nicholas ordered.

"On the grounds of Sexual Battery of a Child, not guilty; on the grounds of Indecent Contact with a Minor, Guilty; on the grounds of Rape of a Child, not guilty; on the grounds of Statutory Rape, not guilty; and on the grounds of Involuntary Deviate Sexual Intercourse with a Child, not guilty."

*I can't fucking believe it! These fucking people think all he did was touch me indecently! Are you fucking kidding me!*

I didn't hear anything else after the verdict. I never saw the jury poled. I didn't hear the judge hand down a sentence of up to three years with credit for time served. I didn't hear shit but a big bag of heroin calling my name.

I couldn't get out of that courtroom and home fast enough. All I wanted was to make a beeline over to Jake's. In the warped sense of reality I was living in, I actually thought he and I bonded over sex that night and he would willingly feed my habit for free. I mean, he let me smoke all I wanted that day and gave me a carryout package to boot. Unfortunately, after my family found it and disposed of it, I was right back to where I started—broke and drugless.

I called Jake as soon as I made it back to the privacy of my room.

"Hey, what's up?" I asked when he answered the phone.

"You got my money?" he asked, with no signs of the Jake I slept with apparent in his tone.

"What money?" I giggled, thinking he was playing.

"The money for all the shit you smoked the other night," he said. "The shit you took with you, too."

I stared at the phone while trying to process what he was insinuating.

"Are you serious?" I finally asked.

"I don't play about my fucking money," he responded. His tone sent shivers up my spine.

"I'll call you back," I told him, barely able to get the words past the lump in my throat.

"Make sure you do that. Don't make me come looking for my four hundred dollars," he said before disconnecting the call.

*Four hundred dollars? Did he really just say four hundred dollars?*

Jake's words and the *Not Guilty* verdicts rang in my ears over and over again. What had I done to deserve this? Apparently, the joke was on me, and someone else wanted in on the action.

As I lay on my bed staring at my reflection in the mirrored doors of my closet, my cell phone rang. The caller ID showed a blocked number. Hesitantly, I answered it.

"Hello?"

At first, no one said anything.

"Hello!" I screamed, getting pissed off.

I had enough shit on my mind without some asshole playing on my fucking phone.

"You and your girl Stacey better watch yourselves. I got proof of your little five-finger discount activity at American Eagle, and if you step out of line, I won't hesitate to send it to the police," the muffled voice threatened.

*Are you kidding me? Today of all days someone wants to play this shit with me? Hell no!*

"Whatever," I responded, clearly doubting their words.

"Oh, you think I'm joking, Ashley Kennedy? Check your messages," they taunted, stressing the fact that they knew exactly who they were talking to. Then, they hung up on me.

As soon as the call ended, my message alert vibrated. Quickly, I opened the icon to a waiting video message. I sat in stunned silence as I watched Stacey grab numerous items from the racks and bring them to the register. The camera then panned to me at the register. It showed me shoving the majority of the items in the bag, while only ringing on the register a few times. The nail in my coffin was the camera came in close enough to see Stacey hand me a twenty-dollar bill for what was probably two hundred dollars' worth of items.

"Fuck!" I screamed.

I threw my phone across the room, shattering the screen. How much worse could my life get?

# ❧Chapter Thirteen❧

Things were going from bad to worse for me. After the conversation with Jake and then the anonymous phone call and video, I tried reaching Stacey, but her phone kept going to voicemail. Finally, I reached out to Dawn. I hadn't seen much of her since this shit with my father started.

"Hey, Ash, what's up?" she said when she answered.

I breathed a sigh of relief. If anyone could help me, it was Dawn.

"I got myself in some serious shit and I need your help," I told her.

"What happened?"

"I owe the guy who Stacey and I get our hook-up from a lot of money," I said, fear obvious in my voice.

"Why?" she wanted to know.

"He let me smoke a bunch of his shit while we got busy. Plus, he gave me some to take home. I damn near OD'd behind the wheel of Mom-Mom's car, and when I went to the hospital, they found the rest of the drugs and confiscated them."

"Oh shit, Ash!"

"Yeah, and that's not all. I thought this fool was letting me have it since we had sex, but now, he's telling me that I owe him for all of it!"

"How much?" she wanted to know.

"Four hundred dollars." I started crying as I thought about the amount.

"Damn, Ash. I'm tapped out. I just paid for my own little stash. If only you had called me earlier," she told me.

"It's cool. I'll figure it out."

Once I knew she couldn't help me, I just wanted to get off the phone. She was the reason I was addicted to this shit in the first place. Her and her fucking life-altering parties!

Just as I was about to hang up, she told me, "Hold up."

"Yeah," I said, hopeful she had a solution.

"I can give you a few bags to give back to him. Maybe that will cut your tab down at least."

It sounded far-fetched, but it was worth a try. I was desperate, so anything was better than nothing at the moment.

"Can you come get it?" she asked.

"Yeah, but I have to catch the trolley. Mom-Mom has me on lockdown as far as her car is concerned, and asking Pop-Pop is out of the question."

"Alright. Well, I'll be here waiting for you."

"Thanks, Dawn. I appreciate this," I told her before hanging up.

I grabbed my phone, clearly pissed off about the shattered screen now that I was slightly calmer. I slid it into the back pocket of the peach-colored Capris I slipped on with a white cotton three-quarter-length sleeve top. I decided on a pair of white footies and white low-cut Reeboks just in case I needed to run for the bus or away from somebody for that matter.

I walked up to Baltimore Pike and waited for the 109 bus. It was taking forever, so I started walking, checking behind me every couple seconds in case it popped up. Five blocks into my walk, I saw it coming. I ran half a block to the stop on the corner across from the Pizza Hut. I was clearly out of breath and immediately felt a bit of regret for forcing Stacey, who wasn't as athletic as me, to run for the trolley that day.

I walked to the rear of the bus and stood by the back door for the ten-minute ride to Dawn's.

I felt like I was in the Penn Relays running one of the baton races. I didn't bother to stay at Dawn's; I went in, got what I needed, and left back out.

As I dropped the four baggies of powder she gave me into my backpack, my hands began to shake. The feel of the soft powder beneath my fingertips felt like heaven to me. I wanted to puncture one of those bags, stick my finger inside, scoop a nice little mountain of powder out, and suck it up my nostril. The only thing stopping me was the thought of Jake coming after me with the gun I saw that day Max and Wayne showed up.

The 109 to 69th Street Terminal showed up shortly after I crossed Baltimore Pike and sat on the bench at the bus stop. I rode it down to the 102 Sharon Hill trolley and made the connection. All the way to Jake's, my fingers played with those bags of powder. I licked my lips more times than L.L. Cool J. I wanted to taste that shit as bad as a person stranded on the desert wants a drop of water. I couldn't get to his place fast enough. Once again, I didn't bother calling; I'd rather negotiate in person.

When he opened the door, he looked just as pissed as he did the last time I showed up uninvited.

"Hey," I said, smiling up at him.

I was hoping he'd recall our sexcapades and cut me a little slack. No such luck.

"You got my money?" he asked, sounding as harsh as he had on the phone.

"No," I answered with a shaky voice.

"Then why the fuck are you here?"

"I have something else," I said, reaching in my bag for the bags of powder.

"If it ain't my money, you can keep it."

"Don't be like," I said.

I dropped them on the bar and tried to caress his muscular arm, but he jumped out of my reach as he looked down at my peace offering.

He laughed wickedly. "What the fuck is that?"

"Heroin. I thought I could give some back and then pay you the rest of the money as soon as I can get it. Graduation is coming up; I'm sure I'll get some money," I told him.

"Are you serious?"

"Yes," I responded.

"Look, Ashley, I don't know where you got that shit from, but I know it's not what I gave you. Now take that shit and sell it, smoke it, whatever the fuck you want to do with it. I don't care. Just bring me my money."

"Jake, I don't have four hundred dollars, and I almost OD'd the night I left here, and my family found the drugs," I rambled until he cut me off.

"Did you tell anybody where you got it from?" he yelled angrily.

"No, I didn't," I screamed back at him.

He grabbed a couple tissues from the coffee table and threw them in my direction. Then he scooped up the bags of powder and dropped them in my backpack.

"What are you doing?" I asked as I blew my nose.

"Take this shit with you and don't come back until you have four hundred dollars cash for me. Do you understand?"

I looked at him, shaking my head that I did. I was so disappointed in him. I couldn't understand why he was being such an asshole. Then he got a phone call, and I think I figured it out. He actually had one of those landline phones with an answering machine that recorded the call. While he was busy trying to rush me out of his place, Max left a message when Jake didn't pick up.

"You better have all our money, Jakey boy, at the end of the week...or else."

A very sinister laugh preceded the dial tone.

"Get my money," Jake informed me before slamming the door in my face.

I walked back up Lansdowne Avenue to the trolley bawling my eyes out. Finally becoming aware that people were staring at me, I cleaned my face and got myself under control.

I boarded the trolley when it arrived and went all the way to the back. I sat and stared at the window, barely noticing the scenery or the stops as they floated by. The only reason why I didn't miss my stop was because the operator called out Baltimore Pike, alerting me that my stop was next.

I got off the trolley and walked inside the playground where Timmy and I would play. I sat on one of the swings made for kids older than him but younger than me and slowly began to push myself with my feet.

*How did my life turn to shit like this? I was a good kid growing up. I just couldn't escape the nightmares of what Johnny did to me. Then Mike raped me and it was downhill from there. I couldn't get myself together with the help of one substance or another. Then that night at Dawn's changed things forever. Heroin made everything better. It turned the rain into sunshine; pain into pleasure. Today, I finally see it for the destroyer it really is. I've lost time I can never get back with my best friend in the world. My family is devastated by the choices I've made recently. Choices that overshadow the life I once had. I have been described as a talented artist and amazing athlete, as well as an intelligent, loving, kind, caring, and beautiful individual. Where did I go wrong?*

I left the playground feeling more determined than I'd been in a long time to put the demons Johnny created to rest once and for all.

After arriving home, I quietly went up to my room. I sat on my bed and pulled out the spiral notebook I carried with me everywhere. Some pages were ripped, with words scribbled here and there. Rich's name was there with hearts and stars from earlier days when things were good. Then I came across pages of words I could never say to *him*...

*You violated me completely*
*And I was only a child*
*You're just a scumbag*
*And should be sent away, miles and miles*
*I'm pushing you out of my life*
*What you did will always be a part of me*
*You owe me and you will never be able to pay that fee*
*You're in debt and you owe your life to me*
*An eye for an eye*
*You know that analogy*
*Well, you do owe my family something*
*A big apology*
*I could've put your ass in jail*
*All alone, no one to help you*
*But then I thought about the boys*
*And thought, well, what good would that do*

*It would have been an escape for you*
*You don't deserve that much*
*You can suffer, just like me...*

I slammed the book shut and slung it on the floor. I didn't want to waste another minute thinking about Johnny. He had already stolen twelve years of my time; he wouldn't get any more.

*I have to figure out a way to get Jake this money so he'll leave me alone,* I thought as I turned out my light and prayed for one night without the nightmares, the tremors, and all the other shit that came with the two worst things in my life...my dad and heroin.

# ֍Chapter Fourteen֍

"Wake up, Ashley! Let's go."

I opened my eyes to those four pairs of eyes staring at me again.

*Oh shit! What did I do now?* I began panicking as I stared at my family circle minus my baby brother and his dad.

"Get dressed," my mom ordered.

I couldn't quite figure out her tone, but I was truly confused and a little disoriented.

"Where are we going?" I asked no one in particular.

"Just get dressed," Pop-Pop said, trying not to sound as angry as he had been lately.

I gave up trying to get a straight answer out of them and went in the bathroom to brush my teeth and take a quick shower.

Quick didn't adequately describe how fast they rushed me out of the bathroom. I think I beat a Guinness World Record in getting dressed. Before I knew it, we were in the car and on our way to somewhere I had no idea where. I sat in the back of Mom-Mom's car watching the scenery change from a cityscape to rural the further we went.

"Where are we going?" I asked repeatedly during the one-hour ride.

They continued to ignore me and my question went unanswered until we pulled into the circular driveway in front of a red brick building with the words *Kenwood Treatment Facility* high above the door.

I stared at the name trying to grasp the true implication of what it meant. Was this really what I thought it was...a rehab center?

*What the hell is this? An intervention?*

"Let's go," my mom said as she slid out the right rear door.

Aunt Chris climbed out the left side, while Mom-Mom and Pop-Pop got out the front. Everyone stretched their legs and backs, recovering from the lengthy ride while I remained seated in the car.

"Come on, Ash," Aunt Chris leaned in and whispered. "It's for the best."

*Says who?* I wanted to say, but I didn't.

Begrudgingly, I finally climbed out the back seat and followed them inside. My arms were folded in front of my chest, and my bottom lip was poked out. I had the appearance of a spoiled toddler, but I didn't care.

*How dare they bring me here without discussing it with me first?*

My mom and Mom-Mom were speaking with the Latino young girl at the front desk who appeared to be only slightly older than me. She smiled in my direction as my mom pointed me out.

"Come here, Ashley," Mom-Mom called to me.

Still sulking, I walked over to where they stood. She firmly grabbed me by my forearm and pulled me closer to the counter.

"Hi, Ashley. I'm Lila. Welcome to Kenwood."

I gave her a half-hearted wave but didn't bother opening my mouth. Mom-Mom's facial expression let me know she wasn't happy with me.

Lila placed a folder full of forms on the counter and slid a black ballpoint pen on top of it.

"Ashley, if you could take a seat over there at that table and fill out some forms, someone will be right with you."

A kind-looking African-American woman, who appeared to be in her late fifties, emerged from the office behind where Lila was seated and walked over to where my family were sitting in the waiting area.

"Hello, my name is Mrs. Jones," she said, offering her hand to each one of them.

Everyone introduced themselves to Mrs. Jones before turning in my direction. I had just finished answering the last questionnaire and was opening and closing my hands to return circulation to my fingers.

"You must be Ashley," she said as she smiled and extended her hand to me.

"Yes. Hi," I mumbled.

Mom-Mom gave me a *get your shit together* look before replacing the smile on her face when Mrs. Jones turned to address them.

"I know you all took great care in selecting a facility for Ashley, and I assure you that we will take excellent care of her. I know we've gone over the requirements of the program." She looked over at my mom. "But, I'll reiterate them for everyone here."

"Pay attention, Ashley," Mom said when she caught my attention wandering elsewhere.

"Ashley will be unable to receive any visitors for the first seven days," she started before I interrupted.

"Seven days? How long will I be here?" I began to panic.

"The program is fourteen days," Mrs. Jones continued.

*Two weeks! Are they crazy? There's no way in hell I'm gonna stay in here for two weeks. What about the things I need to do on the outside? Graduation, Jake and his money, find out who the hell sent me that threatening video. No! No way! I have too much shit to attend to.*

I guess Aunt Chris knew I was panicking inside, because she slowly moved closer to me and began rubbing my back in the soothing way she always did. I took a few deep breaths and tried to get myself under control. It wasn't like I could take a hit to find that wave of calm heroin brought to my life.

Thinking of heroin brought thoughts of Jake back to the forefront. One good thing about being there for two weeks; it would give me a hideout from Jake until I figured out how to get his money.

*The bags of heroin he refused to take are in my backpack! Where the hell is my backpack anyway?*

"Where is my stuff?" I whispered to Aunt Chris.

"Over there," she whispered back, pointing to my one lone red suitcase.

"Did anyone pack my backpack?"

She shrugged her shoulders. My mom gave me a *shut your mouth and listen* look. Things were no longer in my control, so I just gave up. Mrs. Jones continued with the rules of the program and then gave us a few minutes to say goodbye.

"Don't worry, you'll be home before you know it," Aunt Chris whispered in my ear while hugging me. "What's that?" she asked as we felt the vibration from my cell phone in my back pocket.

"No phones allowed," Mrs. Jones reminded when she saw me pull the phone out.

"I'll hold it for you," Aunt Chris told me.

She removed it from my hands and dropped it in her pocketbook before I could even see who was calling.

It didn't matter. Remembering the cracked screen, I wouldn't be able to tell who it was anyway.

Mom, Mom-Mom, and Pop-Pop each took a moment to speak with me alone.

"Ash, I know you're not happy about this, but it's for the best. I don't want to lose you, baby," Mom said before she began to cry.

It seemed lately that's all she had been doing, and I felt like I owed it to her to try and kick this shit. I hugged her tightly and thanked her for caring enough to bring me there. She cried harder, and Aunt Chris put an arm around her shoulders that revealed the depth of her pain as they moved with each sob.

Mom-Mom had wandered off down the hall where there were plaques on the wall. They were mostly of those who had successfully completed the program. Then there were a few that told a different tale.

"Don't let your story end here, Ashley," she whispered as she felt me next to her.

We both stared at the photo of a young lady not much older than me. It was her obituary. Her passing was recent, and no doubt still fresh in the hearts and minds of her loved ones.

"I won't, Mom-Mom," I said as I stared at the girl who looked eerily similar to me.

"We have to get going." Pop-Pop's voice interrupted our thoughts.

I looked up at him and began to cry.

"I'm so sorry I let you down, Pop-Pop," I managed to say before going into total meltdown.

A group of kids exited a nearby room and passed us in the hallway. I tried to regain my composure, but failed miserably.

He hugged me tightly, and then Mrs. Jones ushered me to my room for the next fourteen days, while Lila walked my family to the front door. I turned in time to see the door close behind them, and that's when I fell apart once more.

Mrs. Jones placed my suitcase on the brown wooden high-back chair and then sat on the bed beside me.

"Ashley, I'm not going to lie to you; this is gonna be hard. You will want to quit this more than you ever wanted to quit doing drugs. My staff and I are here to help you every step of the way. The only requirement is that you want to help yourself, first and foremost."

I looked over at her motherly face and knew why they gave her this job. Her heartfelt concern was evident in her words as well as her gestures of kindness. She hugged me as if we had known one another for years instead of just minutes—sixty to be precise.

She gave me an hour to unpack and get myself together before she took me through the first steps of the program. When she returned, I was taken to meet the doctors on staff that would care for me physically, mentally, and emotionally. Once that prerequisite had been met, I met my Addiction Specialist, Lori.

"Hi, Ashley," Lori, a thirty-something, blonde-haired, blued-eyed young lady said as she approached me while I was walking down the hall toward my room.

"Hi," I replied, not sounding as chipper as she did.

"Rough day?" she asked sympathetically.

"You could say that," I agreed.

"I could say it will get better, but it gets worse before it gets better," she stated honestly.

*How much worse could it get?* I thought. And then I found out.

The rest of the week, I suffered through the pain of withdrawal and the pain of missing my family. I honestly couldn't say which one was worse. The only bright spot was that Lori was right by my side the entire time.

"Don't you ever go home?" I asked her as she wiped sweat from my brow and vomit from my lips with two cloths simultaneously.

"I do, except when I get assigned a patient. Besides, I have no one at home anymore. So, I don't mind being here. It keeps me from being lonely sometimes," Lori admitted sadly.

I wanted to ask her what happened, but it was none of my business. If she wanted to share her story, she would. I, on the other hand, ended up sharing my story a few days before I was scheduled to leave. For the first time, I was able to talk about what my dad did to me without feeling like it was my fault.

Lori stood in the back of the room encouraging me as I talked. Together, we had made it through the worst of the withdrawal symptoms. I had been there twelve days. Sadly, it only took one night for all her work to be for nothing.

"Hey, Evan," I said to one of the kids I had made friends with the last few days.

I found out from Lori that he was twenty years old and his habit was the same as mine— heroin. He was short and stocky with a muscular upper body. A close cut fade with curly dirty-blonde hair on top, two earrings in his left ear, nice lips, and brown bedroom eyes completed his look.

After one of our sessions, I found out he was not there willingly. His family members, unlike mine, didn't love him enough to send him there. He was there by the order of the court. Later, when we got to talk while having refreshments, he told me that he had no intention of stopping.

"Follow me," he told me the next night.

"How did you get it in here? Don't they search you?" I whispered when he showed me a stash he had inside one of his socks.

"Nope," he replied as he closed the door partially and told me to stand watch as he took a quick hit.

Watching him pull that bag of powder out of his sock was like a magician pulling a rabbit out of his hat. I stared in awe like a little kid. I hadn't had a hit since the night I almost OD'd in front of the house. My eyes zeroed in on the specks of powder clinging to the fine hairs sticking ever so slightly out of Evan's nostril. I felt myself involuntarily being pulled in his direction right before I heard Mrs. Jones calling us for dinner.

I ran out of Evan's room like it was a raging four-alarm fire inside that bad boy.

Throughout the entire meal, all I could think of was that powder in Evan's room. Before the night was over, I found myself knocking on his door.

"You want a hit?" he asked when he saw me standing at his door looking lost.

I just nodded my head. I was afraid to hear my voice utter the words.

I left Evan's room and scurried back down the hall, trying to remain unseen. The next morning, I couldn't look Lori in her face. I went to every meeting possible that day. It wasn't that I thought it would help get me back on track; I just wanted to stay busy and away from Evan, Lori, and Mrs. Jones.

*Yeah, I was kidding myself if I thought that one hit was going to be it. I fell off the wagon before I'd been in the seat long enough to fasten my seatbelt.*

My last few nights were the worst. I talked with my mom and Aunt Chris on the phone, telling them how well I was doing, before sneaking off to Evan's room to get high. Our final night together, Evan taught me a new trick—how to use a needle.

"Shit! That was like being hit by a train," I said a little too loudly for the nighttime quiet.

"Shhh, Ash." Evan had taken to calling me by my nickname.

"Sorry." I giggled as the high hit me hard and fast.

"Go lie down before you get us in trouble," he demanded.

"Bye-Bye." I waved as I tiptoed back down the hall to my room. *Oh well, I tried,* I told myself as I closed my eyes and nodded off to another drug-induced sleep.

The next day, Evan and I exchanged numbers before I prepared to leave. He would be leaving later that day, too, so we promised to hook up on the outside. It just so happened that we didn't live that far from one another.

My family arrived to pick me up right after breakfast. I was super giddy, thanks to Evan's hook-up. He slid me a little baggie as we passed one another in the hall while leaving the respective restrooms. I did my hit, then brushed my teeth and washed my face repeatedly before joining the others for breakfast.

Evan was only giving me small hits since I just went through withdrawal. I figured my use had gone undetected, but Lila informed me otherwise as I prepared to leave.

"Ashley!" She called my name as she motioned for me to come over to where she sat behind the front desk.

"Hey, Lila. I'm getting out of here today," I told her as if she didn't know.

"I hope I don't see you back here, Ashley. Even more, I hope your obituary isn't the next one on the wall."

I was shocked to hear her say that.

"Why would you think that?" I asked her.

"Because I know what you've been doing the last couple days," she said, no-holds barred.

"Huh?"

"Listen, Ashley, I know Evan. He's been here repeatedly, and each time, it's the same thing. He always finds someone to party with. This time, it was you."

I just stared at her at a loss for words.

"So long," she said and went back to preparing paperwork for the next addict that walked through the door.

I gave Lori and Mrs. Jones a quick hug, then went to wait for the others in the car.

"Everything okay, Ash?" Aunt Chris asked when she got in the car.

"Yeah. I'm just anxious to get back home. By the way, can I have my phone?"

"We'll talk about it when we get home," she told me.

I was about to ask her why we needed to talk about my phone, but everyone else got in the car. So, I let it go. I laid my head against the back of the seat and closed my eyes. I wanted to pretend that I was taking a nap, but they weren't buying it.

My mom began questioning me about what I'd been doing since they visited me earlier in the week. I told her everything I could remember. Yet, I didn't tell her about the one thing I couldn't forget, which was that I had started using again...and with a needle no less.

# ✀Chapter Fifteen✀

"You did what?" I asked Aunt Chris, trying to remain calm.

"Mom-Mom asked me to get you a new phone since your screen was broken. While I was there, we decided to get you a new number, as well," she repeated, although I heard her the first time.

"Can I have my phone, please?"

"I think you should wait a few days before you start contacting anyone," she told me.

"So you're not gonna give it to me?" I asked her a lot calmer than I felt.

"Not yet," she informed me before dropping the new phone in her bag.

"Okay," I said after taking a deep breath.

"You want to go shopping?" she asked to ease the tension.

I laughed and replied, "Sure."

We decided to bypass Springfield Mall and head to King of Prussia Mall instead. The place was huge, and I never made it through more than two buildings each time I went there. The food court alone was a chore to navigate.

"I'll meet you back here in front of the Abercrombie & Fitch store. Okay, Ash?"

"Okay," I answered, slightly distracted by the fact that I thought I had just seen Jake in a crowd of shoppers.

"Did you hear me, Ash?" she repeated.

"Okay, Aunt Chris. Abercrombie & Fitch. I heard you."

"Alright," she said, then headed in the opposite direction from where I swore I saw Jake.

I turned to see where she was headed, and when I turned back around, Jake was standing right in front of me. He grabbed me by the forearm and pulled me into a nearly empty hallway that led to the restrooms and some employee-only offices.

"Where the fuck have you been and where is my money?" he growled.

He pressed my back against the wall, making it appear to passerby that we were a young couple making out.

"I, I've been in rehab," I told him in a voice that let him know I was scared shitless.

"Look, Ashley, I like you...I really do. Under different circumstances, things would probably have gone another way between us. But, business is business, and I need my money. Max and Wayne are looking for me. I'm getting the fuck out of town, and I need my money, Ashley!"

"Jake, I just got home today. I didn't even know they were putting me in rehab. Please give me a couple days to try and get the money," I cried.

Every time someone walked by, he leaned in like he was kissing me.

"Put your arms around my waist," he commanded.

"Huh?"

"Do it," he said between clenched teeth.

I did as he ordered, and then I knew why. He wanted me to feel the concealed gun tucked in his waistband.

"You feel that?" he asked.

I nodded my head, acknowledging that I did.

"Don't make me use it," he threatened. "You have forty-eight hours to get me my money."

"O...okay," I stuttered.

He finally released the hold he had on me, leaving a red mark where his fingers had gripped my translucent skin too damn tight.

"Answer your fucking phone, too," he said, while walking behind me.

"They took it," I hissed back now that I was in a crowd of witnesses.

"You better find a way to contact me or I will find you," he said before walking off, leaving me ready to piss my pants.

I went to find Aunt Chris. I needed to get out of there ASAP. She was surprised to see me empty-handed when I caught up with her at our favorite store, Victoria's Secret.

"You didn't buy anything for graduation tomorrow? I didn't give you enough money?" she asked.

"I didn't see anything," I lied.

The truth was I had completely forgotten about graduation since I'd been in rehab, and didn't think I'd actually make the ceremony.

"You forgot, didn't you?" she asked. Aunt Chris was always able to read my mind.

"Yeah," I replied, then laughed uneasily. Graduation was the furthest thing from my mind.

"They told your mom you could participate in the ceremony, if you want to."

"Okay, cool," I told her, acting like I was thrilled.

"You want to get some stuff from here? They have some new sweats and those tank tops you like." She knew how much I loved clothes from Vicky's.

"No. Maybe another time. I'm ready to go whenever you are."

Aunt Chris looked puzzled. She knew shopping was my favorite thing to do, so she couldn't understand why I wasn't buying anything.

She picked up a couple of items for a weekend away with Uncle Scott. She paid for them, and then we walked back towards the parking garage. On the way out, I saw Jake standing against a large planter pot in the center of the aisle watching us leave. All the way to the car, I kept turning around to see if he was following us.

"Is something wrong, Ash?"

"No. I just thought I saw someone I knew," I answered, telling a half-truth.

She unlocked the door and then tossed me the keys.

"You want to drive?" she asked.

"No, that's okay," I told her.

"Really?" she said, truly surprised. I never passed up an opportunity to drive.

"I don't know my way from up here too well," I explained.

She seemed to accept my answer. On the ride home, she kept asking me if everything was all right. I assured her it was, that I was just tired and had a lot on my mind. It wasn't a lie. I had to figure out how to get Jake that fucking money before the next night. How the hell was I even going to contact him without my phone?

Thank God, Aunt Chris must've read my mind. When we got home, she reached in her tan Nine West bag and handed my phone to me.

"Maybe this will cheer you up."

"Thanks, Aunt Chris," I said, breathing a heavy sigh of relief.

"Use it wisely, Ashley," she warned before leaving me and heading home to her husband.

I ran upstairs to my room and called the number Evan gave me.

"Yo, who's this," he asked when he answered.

"It's Ashley," I responded.

"Ashley?" he said like he had forgotten me already.

"From Kenwood," I reminded him.

"Oh shit! Hey, Ash! What's up?"

"Nothing much. I'm in kind of a bind, Evan. Do you know someone who will buy a Wii and some games, It's only slightly used."

"For how much?" he asked with a chuckle.

"Two-fifty," I said, not wanting to go too high but wanting to get as much money as I could.

"I don't have that much, but I can give you one-fifty and a couple bags of powder. You can sell that shit."

I thought about it for a few minutes and then accepted Evan's terms. I was sure I could find someone to buy the powder. However, it turned out to be a lot harder than I expected. For one thing, I had a hard time trying to remember people's phone numbers that I knew fucked with that shit.

*Damn, I really need my old phone with my numbers in it. But, what good would it do you with a broke screen, dumbass?* I scolded myself.

I pulled out my computer, logged on to Facebook, and started sending messages to people on my page that I knew got high.

*What the fuck! Where are the junkies when I needed them?*

Evan and I made the exchange later that night after everyone was asleep. I tried once more, then decided to call it quits for the night. Tomorrow was graduation, and I intended to be there. Maybe I could finally catch up with Stacey's ass.

As I laid out my outfit that I planned to wear under my cap and gown, I thought about seeing Mia at graduation. I decided I would tell her all about everything I'd been going through. I needed my best friend in my life, and I was going to make sure she knew it. We had wasted too much time apart.

First things first, I had to break ties with Dawn and Stacey. They were both heavily into drugs, and I'd never get off of them if I didn't separate myself from those two. More importantly, I had to get the monkey off my own back.

Suddenly, I remembered the bags of heroin Dawn gave me to give to Jake. I searched my room for my backpack. Finally, I spotted it in the bottom of my closet next to boxes of sneakers I barely wore.

*Maybe I can sell them, too,* I thought as I checked the backpack for the three bags of powder.

"Bingo!" I yelled and then covered my mouth, praying no one came to investigate why I was screaming.

Those three bags plus the two I got from Evan made five. If I sold them at twenty dollar a pop, I could pay off Jake. The promising thought of finally having the money to pay Jake and get him out of my life was enough to send me to bed with a smile on my face.

I was awakened by the bright sunshine streaming in my window. I put my hand up to shield my eyes from the sudden intrusion on my sleep. Between the blinding rays, I saw my mom's smiling face.

"It's graduation day," she sang.

Her good mood was suddenly contagious. I jumped up and twirled around the room like a prima ballerina, one of the only sports I never tried.

"Get ready and I'll drop you off," Mom said and left me alone in my room.

I grabbed my towel and padded down the hall towards the bathroom. The plush carpet they had installed in my absence quieted my footsteps.

I brushed my teeth and then pulled the clear plastic shower cap over my hair before stepping into the steamy shower. I soaped up my entire body, and for the first time, I didn't feel ashamed. My body had always been a constant reminder of the abuse I suffered at the hands of my dad and the other boys in my life.

*Today is the end of that era of my life. Tomorrow I begin a new chapter,* I told myself as I rinsed off and stepped out of the warm water.

I wrapped the towel tightly around my water-covered body and ran back to my room. I dried off, moisturized my upper and lower limbs, and put on my underclothes.

"I'm glad to see that rash has begun to clear up," Mom-Mom said as she walked into my room.

She handed me a small box. I opened it, and inside was a gold chain with a heart attached. Immediately, I felt bad as I recalled a similar necklace that I stole from my mom's jewelry box when I needed money to get a hit.

*I'm gonna buy her a new one,* I vowed, although I knew I could never replace the sentimental value it held. Pop-Pop had bought one for her and one for Aunt Chris.

Shaking off the sad thought, I thanked Mom-Mom for the thoughtful gift. I turned and faced forward, watching her place it around my neck as I stared at our reflection in the mirror. Then, she left me to finish getting ready.

I plugged in my thermal curler and added a few spiral curls to the ends of my normally straight locks. Staring at my reflection as I released the last curl, I didn't know how I was even around to celebrate this day after all I'd been through. I was certainly thankful.

I slipped the purple and gold graduation gown over the nude-colored strapless mini dress that I picked out months ago. Once dressed, I headed downstairs. Pop-Pop told us to come outside for a few photos before we headed over to Villanova University's gym for the ceremony.

They dropped me off at the student entrance and went to park the car.

"Meet us out front right here, Ashley," my mom said before they pulled away.

I waved my hand in the air to acknowledge I heard her and then I went in search of my classmates. I noticed a few people dabbing their eyes with tissues; I assumed they were just happy to be getting out of school and into the real world. Boy was I in for a rude awakening.

"What's going on?" I asked the kid standing in line in front of me.

"You haven't heard?" he began before being shushed by one of the teachers.

*Heard what?*

It was time to march in and take our seats so the ceremony could begin. As we were walking, I searched the crowd for Dawn, Stacey, and most importantly, Mia. I finally made eye contact with Mia, and she gave me a big-ass smile. It warmed my heart, and I mouthed the words, *I love you, Budd,* to her. She cracked a Cheshire cat grin and mouthed,

*Right back at you, Budd*. Budd had been our private name for each other since we were little. At that very moment, I realized how much I had missed my best friend.

Stacey had been a good friend, too. I continued searching the crowd for her. Since I hadn't participated in any of the rehearsals, I had no idea where anyone was located.

*Oh well, I'm sure I'll catch up with her after the graduation is over.*

We took our seats, and forty-five minutes in, they started calling names. We all stood and took our turn walking on stage to accept our diploma. When Stacey's name was called, I was shocked to see her mother step up on stage.

"Ladies and gentlemen, we'd like to deviate for just a moment from our program while one of our parents who recently lost their child speaks to the student body."

*What! Lost! When?*

I wanted to scream, cry, kick, punch...anything to get someone to tell me this wasn't real.

Instead, I sat there like a zombie as Stacey's mother told everyone about her passing from a drug overdose three weeks ago. Immediately, my mind did the math. The last time I spoke with her was before I went to Jake's looking for a freebie. When I tried reaching her before I was sent to rehab, I kept getting her voicemail. Now I knew why.

*Here I was talking about ending our friendship and my girl is dead. How could I be so selfish? Because you are,* I berated myself.

My tears fell as I thought about the escapades Stacey and I had. My heart was hurting so badly that I wanted to rip it out of my chest. When it was time for me to accept my diploma, I walked up on stage praying I didn't fall on my face. My vision was blurred by the tears I just couldn't seem to stop from falling. The remaining names went by in a blur; then I just followed behind the person in front of me as we marched back out.

As people began coming up to me, I pushed past them in search of Mia. I needed my friend.

"Hey, Ashley." Dawn and Brenda appeared out of nowhere.

"Hey," I said, wiping my eyes.

"Sorry about your girl Stacey," Brenda said.

"Thanks. Did you guys know?"

"Yeah. I tried calling your phone when I found out," Dawn told me.

"I didn't get it," I replied, puzzled.

"Yeah, I know. Your phone was disconnected."

*Shit! I forgot about Aunt Chris changing my number.*

"Yeah, I broke my phone. Aunt Chris bought me a new one and got me a new number."

"Why did she get your number changed?" Brenda questioned.

Not feeling like talking anymore, I just shrugged my shoulders.

"I'll talk to you guys later. I gotta go," I told them, then hurried off to find Mia.

I walked out and saw Mia standing against Mom-Mom's car with the rest of my family. Just like the old days...

She rode home with us, and she and I spent the entire ride in the backseat squished between Aunt Chris and my mom. It didn't matter. We were used to it from all the family trips we took together.

"You coming in?" I asked Mia when we pulled up in the driveway.

"Yeah, for a minute. My mom is on her way to get me. We're going out to eat. You want to come?"

I thought about it, but I didn't have an appetite...at least not for food. Even though Stacey died from an overdose, I still craved a hit to dull the pain her death was causing me.

"I have a lot to tell you," I told Mia as we lay across my bed staring at ourselves in the mirrors on the closet.

"Ashley and Mia...together again," Mia said.

"Did you hear me, Mia?"

"Yeah. Tell me tomorrow, okay? I don't want to ruin this moment. We can talk about it later."

"Okay," I agreed.

A few minutes later, Mia's mother showed up.

"You sure you don't want to come?" Mia asked again.

"No, I'm fine. I'll see you tomorrow, okay?"

"Okay. Bye, Budd," she said, hugging me.

"Bye." I waved as she got in the car.

"Hey," she yelled out the window once she rolled it midway down.

"What?"

"Isn't tomorrow your grandmom's birthday?"

"Yep. Good memory," I told her.

"How many birthdays have we spent with her?"

"A lot," we said in unison as her mother pulled off.

"Ashley, you want something to eat?" my mom yelled from the kitchen.

"No, I'm not hungry."

I went upstairs and tried to come to terms with Stacey's death.

"Knock, knock," Aunt Chris said as she stood in my doorway.

"Come in," I told her.

"You okay, Ash? I'm sorry about Stacey," she said as she plopped down beside me on the bed.

"I just don't understand." I began to cry.

"We never do when someone leaves so unexpectedly."

She let me cry, and once I got myself together, she told me to come downstairs for a minute.

My mom, stepdad, and Timmy were about to leave. I was so distraught about Stacey that I hadn't even realized Timmy and Jimmy were there.

Timmy jumped in my arms and planted wet sloppy kisses on my face. I took my hand, balled it up against his belly, and shook it so it would tickle him. He just laughed and laughed.

"Here, Ash," Mom said, handing me a card.

Mom-Mom, Pop-Pop, Jimmy, Uncle Scott, and Aunt Chris all slid their cards on the table in my direction.

"Thank you," I said repeatedly as I removed various denominations of money from each card.

I easily calculated I had enough to pay Jake off.

"Pop-Pop, can you take me to the bank to deposit it tomorrow?" I asked, looking for a way to begin to repair our relationship.

"Sure," he said and smiled at me.

I missed that smile. Seeing it made me believe things would be all right.

About an hour later, my mom and Jimmy prepared to take a sleeping Timmy home.

"See you tomorrow, Ash," she said, placing a kiss on my forehead.

"Okay," I said as I walked them to the door.

Aunt Chris and Uncle Scott were the next to leave.

"See you guys tomorrow," they said, too.

"Congrats, Ash. I'm proud of you," Uncle Scott expressed.

"Me, too," Aunt Chris said as she hugged me tightly.

Finally, they left, and I headed upstairs.

"Wow, it's after midnight. Where does the time go?" I heard Pop-Pop ask as he plopped down in his favorite chair in the living room.

I backtracked halfway down the steps and leaned over the banister.

"Happy birthday, Mom-Mom. I love you," I shouted to her as she sat at the dining room table sitting my cards up on display.

She smiled back and replied, "I love you, too."

"Love you, Pop-Pop."

"Love you, too, Ash. See you in the morning."

"Nine o'clock?" I asked.

"Nine o'clock," he confirmed.

I went in my room and flopped down on the bed as I set the alarm clock for our trip to the bank. I was about to lock my door, but then decided not to. There was no longer anything to be afraid of. At least there wouldn't be after I gave Jake his money the next day. I decided to put the money in the bank so no one would realize I didn't have it. I'd try to replace it before they found out. It was a small price to pay to get Jake off my back and out of my life.

Something wasn't sitting right with me. I decided to call Jake before he came looking for me. I picked up the phone, but instead of calling him, I dialed the number to the voicemail of my old number.

*"Ash..."*

I heard Stacey's voice calling out to me, and it sent chills up my spine.

*"Ash, I told Jake to leave you alone. He told me about the money. I told him I'd report him to the cops if he didn't stop hounding you. He said he'd call it even. He even gave me a freebie so I wouldn't rat him out. It must've been some bad shit,"* she said as her words began to slur.

Tears ran down my face as I heard my girl actually dying on my voicemail.

*"Ash....Jake gave me..."*

Her voice trailed off, and it sounded as if the phone hit the floor.

I pressed the end button. I couldn't take anymore. My girl died trying to stand up for me. Here I was talking about breaking ties with her and she was dead...because of me.

Unable to deal with this revelation, I paced my room, walking back and forth in front of the mirror on the dresser. Then around the bed and back to the door, each time catching my reflection in the mirror. My reflection taunted me; it blamed me for all kinds of shit. Before I knew it, I pulled out the bags of powder I hadn't sold. I opened one and snorted the entire bag. As time ticked by on the clock, I grew more and more restless. I opened another bag, this time locating the kit Evan made me in rehab to shoot up whenever I got the urge for the big bang.

I called Jake's phone and waited for him to pick up.

"Who is it?" he asked when he answered, not bothering with being polite.

"It's Ashley, muthafucka." The words came out slurred and not at all intimidating like I planned.

"You got my fucking money?" he growled.

"You killed my friend."

For a moment, there was silence on the other end of the phone. I wondered if he heard me.

Then he said, "So what? The bitch should've minded her own business...coming here threatening me. She got what she deserved!"

I couldn't believe he had admitted that he killed Stacey. Now I knew it was my fault.

"I hope you're calling to say you got my money, because time's up. If I don't get my money by noon, I'll be paying your family a visit!"

"What! How dare you threaten them," I cried.

"It's not a threat, sweetheart."

"You're gonna get your money," I said as I pushed the plunger deep into my vein, releasing the liquid courage.

"I better or—"

His words were cut off as I heard two pops.

*Was that gunshots?*

"Hello? Jake?"

There was no response, only a dial tone.

I was high as a kite. My heart felt like it was going to pop out of my chest. I saw my spiral notebook sticking out from under my pillow. I tried numerous times to pull it out before my fingers finally grabbed the spiral ring. As I pulled it closer, I flipped it open. I tried to lift my pen that was stuck between the pages, but I couldn't. It was too heavy.

I gave in to the feeling consuming me. I couldn't fight it anymore.

The words on the notebook page on display was my final statement to the world.

*Alive with the deafening sound of silence*
*On a winding path leading nowhere*
*Brightly lit by eternal darkness.*
*The smallest thing inside that deepest soul*
*Falling heels over head into the shallowest abyss.*
*All of this shortly after unmistakable bliss.*
*Followed by the Universe's unforgiving time shift.*
*Leaving what's left of the mind*
*Flipped and Scattered*
*Torn and Battered,*
*Forcing the deepest of the unconscious to realize that*
*Nothing ever mattered.*
*The world ending to begin,*
*Resetting itself on a backwards spin.*
*Upside Down.*
*Tossing a resisting lifeline into that*
*Booming Silence*
*Misguided by the*
*Darkest Shining.*
*That simply complex path*
*Ceasing to wind*

# HEROIN HEARTBREAK

*Following the lead of*
*Ever reversing time.*
*Beginning to rewind,*
*Backwards*
*Through what's left of the*
*Bewildered Mind.*
*The Universe giving a sign,*
*A chance to undo the largest mistake of*
*Human Kind.*
*Forcing you to rethink your*
*Decision,*
*The objective of your overall*
*Mission.*
*What is it that you were missing?*
*Decisions out of your control,*
*Fate forcing your submission.*
*The World forcing you to listen*

# ◈Epilogue◈

"Ashley! Ashley! Wake up! You got in! You got in!" Mom-Mom screamed, informing me I'd been accepted to the college of my dreams, Alabama University, the family alma mater.

Opening the door to my room, ready for me to share in her excitement, Mom-Mom comes face to face with my lifeless body.

"Noooo!"

The scream that escapes her mouth I don't get to hear.

I am still in the clothes from last night. My body is rigid and cold; there is foam hanging from my mouth. My arm is outstretched, ready for the next injection that is no longer needed. I already had more than my weakened heart could stand. The evidence is there beside me for all to see. My final moment; my moment of weakness on display.

She continues to call my name, willing me to open my eyes. Eyes that will no longer see another day. Eyes that no longer have to look around for the monsters that have been hiding in the closet for the past twelve years.

She doesn't want to leave me alone, but she must to go find Pop-Pop. I'll be okay. I wish I realized that I wasn't alone all these years. If only I had realized that my family would protect me from the monsters I feared.

She returns with Pop-Pop by her side. He's always been there—for her, for me, for all of us. I wish I could be there for him right now; for both of them...for all of them. My leaving is the final blow that they will not recover from.

Pop-Pop holds me, rocks me, begging me to come back. He tells me that he is sorry for not believing me, not seeing the pain I hid so well. I want to reach up and touch his face, to tell him it's okay...that it's not his fault.

The paramedics come, the police come, and with them is my heartbroken mother. She is wrapped in a blanket of denial. She looks at my lifeless form and begs someone to wake her from this nightmare. She refuses to accept that she will not see me smile again. She won't hear my voice calling her name. That she will not get to see me play with my little brother. That she will not see me walk down the aisle to get married. That she will not hold a grandchild in her arms that was born unto me and the man of my dreams. No, she does not accept any of this as she removes me from the grip Pop-Pop still has on me.

"Ashley, I promise I will make him pay for this," she whispers into my ears that no longer hear her words of comfort.

Punishing the man that created the life and stole it away becomes her mission as she holds me tight and kisses me one last time before I am taken from her arms. The courts were too lenient on him; she won't stop 'til justice is served.

Before the police begin their investigation, Mom-Mom re-enters the room. She brushes her fingers through my hair like she used to when I was little. She doesn't say anything at first. For once, there are no words from either of us, just a moment of silence to say our goodbyes.

I wish I could tell her how much I love her. How sorry I am that I chose today, her birthday, to lose my battle with this disease. She will never be able to enjoy another birthday after this; the day will always be tainted with the sadness of my passing.

When she has had her time with me, the police step in and begin to process the scene. The paramedics have left; there was nothing for them to do when they arrived. Too much time had passed since I drew my final breath.

Aunt Chris is out of town with Uncle Scott; they don't make it back to witness this horrible scene. It's probably for the best, although the long drive home is one she will probably never forget. I'm thankful for all the wonderful times we have shared, and hopefully, those memories will get her through the difficult days ahead.

Timmy doesn't get to see me again, but I know everyone will make sure he doesn't forget me. In his short life, we built a bond that can't be broken, and one day, he will know all about his big sis from all those whose lives I have touched. I just regret that I will not get to see him grow up into the wonderful young man he is destined to be.

July 20<sup>th</sup>

Today I am being laid to rest. My struggles are over; finally, I am at peace. My ceremony is private. There's only family and a few select friends who are invited. One by one, people get up and say wonderful things about me. They don't speak of my struggles; they only talk about the Ashley they knew.

My best friend Mia steps to the microphone. She introduces herself, although most of them know her, and tells everyone about the Ashley she knew.

"When Ashley and I first met, we didn't like each other. Actually, I didn't like her. I told her that I wasn't interested in being friends, but the truth was I wanted to be just like her. She was amazing, and even in the first grade, everyone knew it.

"She refused to believe that I wasn't interested in making friends. Every time she came to school, I bullied her. Until one day she stood up for herself. After that, we became the best of friends.

"I looked forward to seeing her at school, hanging with her on the weekends, and spending summer at the shore. There will not be a day that goes by that I won't remember her for the best friend she was."

She says a few more words and then comes down and places a kiss on my forehead.

"I'll miss you, Ashley. Rest in peace, Budd."

VANESSA M. KIRBY

*In Loving Memory of Amber M. Masters*
*4/19/94 - 7/16/12*

When Amber was born, the first thing you noticed was her big brown eyes. I remember looking through the glass at the hospital and her staring back at me. I fell in love with her before she was even born. However, seeing her for the first time made me love her even more. I knew that her and I would become very close.

She was such a smart little girl. She started reading at a very young age. She started drawing at a young age as well. In second grade, she had to do a book report. She drew the cover of the book that she read on her report. The drawing was so amazing that her teacher did not believe that she drew it. My sister went to school and had Amber re-draw the picture in front of the teacher to prove she didn't trace it.

She had such amazing talent! There was nothing that Amber couldn't do. She was blessed with looks, brains and talent. She was so smart that she was able to finish high school five months before the rest of her class. She was an amazing athlete! She enjoyed playing basketball, volleyball and softball. She was a natural talent at everything she did. She never seemed to struggle with anything…..accept for her addiction.

She had hopes of getting into the University of Alabama. There was an issue with some of her classes which delayed her acceptance to the University. One week to the day after she passed, we received her acceptance letter. I can't help but wonder if knowing she got accepted would have been enough to cure her of her addiction.

Heroin is a disgusting drug that ruined my family. Having Amber ripped out of our lives is something my family will never get over. We never got the chance to say goodbye. It is very difficult to watch my sister and parents struggle with Amber's death.

Amber has three younger brothers who will not get the chance to grow up with their big sister. They will only have memories of her the rest of their lives. They are being cheated out of seeing first hand what an amazing person their sister was.

I hope that this book helps those struggling with addiction. It may also open up others eyes for warning signs which my family missed until it was too late.

Thank you Vanessa for all your hard work on this book. You are an amazing person and my family is very lucky to have you in our lives! We love you.

Nicole (Amber's aunt)

Made in the USA
Middletown, DE
28 August 2022